GLAMOUR AND TURBULENCE—
I Remember Pan Am, 1966–91

Aimée Bratt

VANTAGE PRESS
New York

FIRST EDITION

Published by Vantage Press, Inc.
516 West 34th Street, New York, New York 10001

Manufactured in the United States of America
ISBN: 0-533-11972-3

Library of Congress Catalog Card No.: 96-90242

0 9 8 7 6 5

To the former
Pan Am
flight attendants

Contents

The following is an account of how I perceived what it was like flying for Pan Am in the past. It is in no way intended to reflect or relate to the situations or conditions existing in the airline industry today.

1

Hired by Pan Am—A Dream Come True

Stockholm, Sweden, 1965

Almost thirty years ago I was interviewed by Pan American World Airways in one of the hotel suites of the Grand Hotel in wintery Stockholm, December 1965.

At that time, being a Pan Am stewardess was truly one of the most desirable occupations you could land. When I saw the ad in the paper, I knew there were going to be hundreds and hundreds of applicants. I think they needed only twenty girls who were willing to relocate to the United States. You had to be attractive, "outgoing," and relatively well-educated, i.e., they preferred you to have had two years of college or the equivalent or more and speak at least one foreign language, in addition to fluent English. They wanted girls from "good families," and certainly if you had connections to Pan Am it helped. The competition was rumored to be so intense that one was advised, or it was suggested, to go all the way to New York to be interviewed, where it would be easier to get hired since there you stood out as a minority. There were articles written in magazines about the glamorous lifestyle of the Pan Am stewardess. Why Pan Am? Because it was the most international and renowned airline in the world, the pioneer in aviation.

Everywhere the Blue Ball was displayed on billboards and ads, matched only by the Coca-Cola sign (and, in the remote parts of the Yemen desert, by Singer sewing machines!).

Pan Am had an aura, an image, a logo, and a sophistication that none of the other airlines possessed. Although I wanted very much to be an airline stewardess (that *was* the term used at the time) flying for any airline, Pan Am was the only one I applied to and really wanted. Any other would have been second best.

I thought I had a decent chance, because I had grown up in many different countries and had a diplomatic background. My father at the time was the Swedish envoy in Teheran, serving Iran and Afghanistan, and that was one area Pan Am flew to.

I spoke English well, in addition to Swedish, French, and German. I was only twenty-two, but I had had a number of short-term jobs. After graduating from secondary academic schooling, the so-called "studenten" in Sweden, I worked as a secretary for a short while and then on to Paris in order to learn French better, where I worked as a model in one of the fashion houses at Rue St. Honoré for at least ten months. I then returned to Stockholm to go back to school, a commercial institute, where I graduated after one year and got a job in advertising, marketing products, and traveling all over Sweden. It was fun for a while, but I'd known since I was a little girl that I wanted to fly. Also, I did not want to remain in Sweden, where I felt confined.

So I went up to the Grand Hotel one very cold morning for the interview. December was so cold in Stockholm at the time that women were wearing woolen knee-long underpants under their skirts. I was worried that they might look too bulky and that I would not appear slim and trim enough for this glamour job!

I had on an emerald green haute couture suit (acquired in Paris from the fashion house I had worked in), and in the bathroom of the Grand Hotel off came the bloomers and heavy boots and on went a pair of nice high-heeled shoes. There was a "real" stewardess in there in an immaculate blue uniform, who gave me a cool glance. She looked like she belonged in places like these; the Grand Hotel was indeed a very elegant old hotel. I was very envious.

The waiting room was crowded with girls, who looked like they were there for some kind of modeling audition. It really was very intimidating, and everybody was extremely serious for some reason, almost pompous, no smiles.

When I was called, the interviewer, a man, led me into a little room. While I was walking in, I knew he was examining my legs quite thoroughly, because I had seen him do that to all the others. I thought it was a little too obviously done, but it did not bother me. (This was 1965, remember.)

I felt fairly comfortable during the interview, because I was used to the American way of communicating. It was all quite relaxed and informal, especially compared to Swedish job interviews. I was told to come back in the afternoon. The first "weeding out" had been accomplished.

When I returned, only a few girls were present. At my second interview my skin was closely examined and I was asked to walk a few steps to the corner of the room. There were three ladies this time, who asked me, "Why do you want to become a stewardess?" Did I know that it was a hard job? Did I like people?

They got a rather superficial impression of me, I'm

sure, but the fact that I spoke several languages and had grown up in the foreign service seemed to be enough. I was also not bowlegged, I did not have pimply skin or a shrill voice, nor was I six feet tall (unacceptable for stewardesses).

There was going to be a waiting period of six months before I knew if I had the job. One of the ladies asked me to bring a little present to someone in Teheran who was working there for Pan Am. I was going to visit my father anyway (my parents were divorced), so I gladly did her the favour, thinking maybe it was a sign that I already had been accepted. It turned out to be true, of course. However, to be hired by Pan Am coming all the way from Stockholm via Teheran was to be a lot harder than I had imagined.

In Teheran I waited every day for a letter. I was so nervous and eager to get this job that I could think of nothing else. Here I was, going to cocktail parties and black-tie dinner parties, dressed in silk, crepe, and chiffon, accompanied by my father and his British wife, Sonia, a very poised but imperious lady. I was surrounded by wealthy Iranians and members of the various diplomatic corps, dined on pearl grey Iranian caviar and drank champagne, and lived at the Swedish Embassy, served by servants and all. I was driven around in the embassy car on shopping rounds with Sonia, the Swedish flag flapping on the hood of the car! I even had a job, as some kind of secretary for the Swedish ballbearing company SKF, in addition to a few modeling appearances for an Iranian fashion designer who paid me with a dress! You see, money was too lowly! For six months I did all this in Teheran, but all I really was interested in was the acceptance letter from Pan Am.

Now I had already seen the world. I grew up in East Africa, namely Ethiopia. For the most formative years of my life, ten to sixteen, I had had the great experience of being part of what was the adventure of growing up in the fifties in Africa. It was a time of great beauty, romance, the wild East African nature, and the animals. Ethiopia is a mountainous land with alternating hot and rainy seasons. The colors of the eucalyptus trees and the red earth are so stark and the smells so fragrant. We would sit at night out in the wilderness around a campfire surrounded by the strange howls of the hyenas and other animals, drinking gin and tonics and singing songs and talking about how lucky we were to be there. But that had been a long, long time ago.

Earlier, I also grew up in Berlin. It was 1950, and I remember the first time I saw ruins, what a shock it was. I was eight years old. Emaciated little children with old faces were glaring at us as we were driving by in East Berlin. On our way from Sweden to Berlin, we travelled by car, and something happened that I will never forget. How terrified I was! It is etched in my memory.

We had taken the wrong road, which turned out to be a dirt road for East German refugees. At the border they held my father for three hours, questioning him about who he was and what he was doing on this road. He spoke Russian fluently, which helped the situation, because the border patrol was Russian here in the Russian sector. Friendly they were not, but we were finally released, after it was proven that he was only the future Swedish consul general on his way to his new post! And this was also after two menacing-looking armed soldiers came down from a tree with their guns pointed at us!

In addition to the above mentioned, I had travelled extensively all over central Africa, as well as having spent three months in South Africa when my parents were there. I went by myself, at seventeen, on a cargo ship with only twelve other passengers from Copenhagen through the Bay of Biscay all the way to Cape Town, a wonderful journey.

When I applied to Pan Am, it was not so much that I wanted to see the world, but I did want to continue a way of life I had been used to. Flying was the right occupation for me. There was also a certain freedom that few other jobs could provide, not nine to five but plenty of flexible schedules (especially in those days), and the time off you had! I knew it would be a hard job, although not in the way I had envisioned it. The emotional labour was something else that came later as a rather alarming discovery. People kept telling you over and over again, whether they were informed or not—I suspect in order to make some kind of impression on you—that the job was *not* glamorous.

They could not have been more wrong!

2

The Pan Am Indoctrination

While waiting in Teheran for the letter (I still did not know if I had been accepted), I would periodically receive instructions from the airline to go for medical exams. You had to have excellent physical health, twenty-twenty vision, etc. That was part of the prerequisites for being hired. They had employed a local doctor there, an Iranian. Unfortunately, he did not set a good example for Pan Am. He was a rather crude individual who spoke of the airline as "my baby" and treated me with misplaced familiarity, calling me "honey" and "sweetheart." It sounded extremely vulgar. He was unethical, which was worse. I must have had five different medical checkups, four of them unnecessary, i.e., he kept telling me to come back week after week for the same tests. He made up all sorts of symptoms, so that for a while there I thought I *was* sick. He would take my pulse sitting, standing, walking, and even tried to make me run around in his office for more pulse taking! Then he would bill Pan Am for all the trouble. I later learned that he was known for his dubious practices. Why he and the others who took advantage of Pan Am over the years were not fired, I'll never understand.

The letter finally came, but it sent me into a panic. I was to report immediately to the headquarters in Miami. They gave me one day! I had to take the first Pan Am flight out of Teheran to Miami via New York. However, there was a little problem. I had no visa, and the American Embassy was closing in one hour.

I dashed over there (the chauffeur took me in the car) a few minutes before closing time. I think if I had been too late, I might not have been sitting here writing. Pan Am did not accept late-comers (they probably viewed it as indicating future tardiness in the job); and if you did not show up on time "for duty," it was interpreted as a voluntary "no-show" and you lost the job. Similarly, later under employment, if you for some reason would be unavailable for contact for three days or more, it was termed a "voluntary resignation."

I managed to get my U.S. visa, and the next day I was on my way to Miami, not very well prepared for the ensuing revelations. For some reason I was seated in first class (probably by a well-meaning ground agent), and this was not viewed with sympathy by my future coworkers. The crew informed me of the fact that a new-hire or "trainee" did not sit in first class! But there I was anyway and afraid to move.

I later timidly asked the purser, a seasoned middle-aged man of Italian-American descent, what the job was like. He did not answer the question but told me matter-of-factly that I would spend the first year flying back and forth to Bermuda, based in New York. Well, he turned out to be wrong.

As far as the job was concerned, I learned that the actual work on the plane was not the hard part. A stewardess pointed to the galley and said, with a gesture of the hand, "That's easy! It is the time change that will get you!" And this time someone was going to be right! Jet lag fatigue, year after year, is crushing. My mother said once,

"You know how tired you feel after a flight; it's no different for a flight attendant."

Upon my arrival in Miami, what followed was actually a bit of a rude awakening. We were treated a little like high-school students. The atmosphere was patronising. We were four to a room in a "Miami Airways Motel." At the outdoor pool were a variety of idle men, lounging around for the sole purpose of watching us, the new-hires. It was impossible anyway to get a date with any of us since we were subjected to the strictest rules, not allowed out after ten at night, and we also had an enormous amount of material to study. The food at the Miami Airways Motel was abominable. I actually lost weight. Never in my life had I tasted such blandness. For the first time ever, I met a truly obese person. It made such an impression on me because I had never seen anything like it, and what amazed me was that his condition did not seem to bother him.

Airplanes were flying overhead all the time. Very stressful. After my long trip from Teheran and all this so-called culture shock, I ended up the first day in bed with such an attack of migraine that an injection of some form of morphine had to be administered in my arm. I recovered and started to adapt. We were to be indoctrinated into the so-called "Pan Am image," and that was very serious business.

The training was conducted at high-speed by an energetic Irish-American former purser, and it lasted only five weeks (as opposed to three to six months at the European airlines at the time), the last week being a test flight. You were paid for this training and then placed on the line in order to become productive as soon as possible, at first for a six-month probation period, during which you learned everything. You were "on probation" or a "trainee," and in those days you were certainly treated with mild contempt. You could be fired for a small infraction, like not smiling enough for instance. It was just a trial period you had to endure. The training was something I do not look back upon as enjoyable. It was an ordeal.

I don't know how it is possible, but we were glorified and humbled at the same time. We were molded into perfect stewardesses. Like soldiers in an army we had to cut our hair (it could not touch the collar), lipstick and nail polish had to be red or coral, make-up applied according to regulation, uniform skirt not too tight or too loose, and undergarments were mandatory—full slip, nylon hose, full bra, panties, and girdle—and were checked periodically. The Pan Am uniform was actually great-looking: blue-grey gabardine, a pillbox hat (the fashion of the sixties), black high-heeled shoes, leather over-the-shoulder handbag, and white, white gloves! Some people thought of it as oppressive, but one has to admit it—we had *style!*

The training consisted of one week of jet emergency procedures, another week of service training, another of paperwork and introduction to other departments, like scheduling, the union, etc., and then the all-important grooming regulations, as well as how to handle passengers (which cannot really be taught) and, last, the training flight.

The emergency training at that time consisted of military-style procedures taught with incredible speed. It was jumping into chutes and life rafts (in real water) and learning how to use fire extinguishers, oxygen bottles, megaphones, radio beacons, and all kinds of survival equipment and how to evacuate from aircraft and survive in stormy seas. You learned about decompression, hypoxia, hypothermia, hyperventilation, bleeding, broken bones, heart attacks, even childbirth, and how to administer first aid in all of this. And every single day we had written tests on the material covered, as well as a lot of homework.

The actual service training was very superficial. A first-class service was demonstrated in a mock-up galley, and you got no hands-on experience. This was something you had to learn in flight, and cause for much nervousness. A Pan Am first-class service at that time was quite an elegant presentation, and when you were forced to work the first-class galley, you needed all the help you could get. Cooking roast beef at 35,000 feet in an old-fashioned oven or setting up a cart-by-cart service with silver utensils and linens and china in turbulence is no easy task.

As far as the service was concerned, what took the new-hired by surprise was the incredible speed with which it had to be accomplished in flight. That was never mentioned in training.

"Scheduling" was another novelty to us. How all-important a role this department would come to play we had no idea. How you bid your trips and how you are awarded them is basically what makes or breaks the quality of a flight attendant's life. We were also introduced to "the union," and again, we could not have dreamt what the future would have in store for us.

In training in 1966 we were given inoculation injections. Every other day we had to receive another shot in the arm. Pan Am was flying to a lot of exotic places like India and Africa, so we had to carry our immunization records with us along with passports, alien cards, etc. If you did not have your shots or records up-to-date, you were taken off the flight.

We learned about how to calculate the time difference, the GMT, the twenty-four-hour clock, customs procedures, foreign currency, and all the paperwork connected with flying. It was all quite superficial, though. You *learned* only five percent in training (mostly emergency procedures) and 95 percent on the job flying.

My training flight was a disaster. I was intimidated as well as airsick! I did not work, I could not work, and I was not offered work. The crew just let me sit there. The only thing I learned from it was that crew members spent a lot of time drinking and partying in hotel rooms, in this case London. There were no reports about me, which was a little alarming, since everybody else in my training class got letters stating how wonderfully they had performed!

Well, things finally loosened up for me. I learned to *smile!* And that was the key. In America, you have to smile or at least give the appearance of friendliness. I went further than that. I actually started laughing quite a lot. Doors opened up for me. I was beginning to discover the power of cheerfulness and persuasion. However, I could not relax quite yet or even enjoy my new job fully, because the six-month probation period awaited me. I would be under other people's control for a while, but somewhere in the future I knew that I would have great freedom in this kind of lifestyle.

We graduated at the end of May 1966 with our golden wings on the blue uniforms, white gloves, and pillbox hats with the Pan Am sign displayed on them, posing for a photograph that more than anything demonstrated the "Pan Am image."

It was some ceremony. Champagne was served, and it was said that this was the only time in your lifetime you were allowed to drink "in uniform."

3

"Look Like a Woman; Think Like a Man; Work Like a Horse"

It was a shock. When I first started flying, somebody gave the description of the job wryly as "look like a woman; think like a man; work like a horse." In those days "looking like a woman" vaguely meant being as attractive as possible, "thinking like a man" implied being somewhat unemotional in the performance of the job, and "working like a horse"—well, it was a matter of crowded galley space, impractical working conditions, heavy bending and lifting, and performing safety and service procedures with an incredible speed in flight as well as on the ground. All this was a somewhat rude awakening to a new-hire flight attendant. It would take a lot of practice to perform in these contradictory roles. On one hand, it was expected of you to always look your best, well groomed, with immaculate uniform, clear skin, makeup applied perfectly, shoes shining, hair "regulation" style, even jewelery "regulation" as well as hose and the girdle, which were "checked" before every single flight. If something was not right, you were given a "discrepancy" and not allowed to work your flight. It could have been a too-tight skirt or too-long hair or even a blemish or scar on the skin. For instance, bandages were not allowed. On top of all this was the *smile*. You were supposed to display warmth, gentleness, charm, endless caring for the passenger, never-ending patience in difficult situations, and, above all, an unflappable cheerfulness in dealing with both passengers and other crew members. The all-important teamwork was stressed. "Getting along" with people was essential. Individuals with serious expressions on their faces or with a hint of reserved mannerisms were quickly labeled "cold" and "standoffish" and called into the office to discuss their "attitude." On the other hand, the job required you to be firm, strict, decisive, and aggressive in enforcing all of the federal aviation safety rules. Try to tell an argumentative passenger to stow his overstuffed suitbag in the overhead bin with charm and cheerfulness! Or try to force a drunk passenger in the back of the cabin to sit down and stop throwing cigarette butts on the floor with gentleness. Or try "diplomatically" to convince an insistent passenger that it is strictly prohibited to visit the cockpit in flight due to security measures. Why can you not just tell them, point-blank, that all of this is not allowed, like a cop would do or maybe a nurse or other professional? Because then you run the risk of being accused of "rudeness." This was a service industry, and the customer was always right, even if he refused to sit down when the seat belt sign was illuminated. At the same time it was the flight attendant's responsibility to make sure the passenger got seated. Since you could not physically force him down into his seat, you had to "persuade" with whatever resources you had.

In the midsixties, however, when I started flying, passengers were ever so respectful of airplanes and us, the crew. Flying was an experience and somewhat elitist, and we represented adventure and a certain escapism.

I was based in San Francisco, and my very first flight

was to Tokyo. I was assigned the back galley and was in for a fast lesson. I will never forget that flight. It so happened that of all things, I used to be airsick! As a child I had travelled a lot in cars and on airplanes, and I almost always got sick.

I was well aware of my "handicap" when I applied for this job, and it had been my most serious concern. How would I fly? With or without Dramamine? Drugs were certainly not permitted. You were not even allowed to fly on antibiotics, for fear that being under the influence of any medication, you would perform poorly in an emergency situation.

Well, on this flight my airsickness mysteriously vanished! And as I have stated, this was after being airsick on every single flight in my life. How was it possible that this time I did not even feel a trace of it? The only explanation I can think of is that my fear of making mistakes and general nervousness over the job were greater than my airsickness! And in addition, I had never worked harder in my life either.

This was a Boeing 707 with about 120 passengers in economy and twenty or so in first class. We were six flight attendants, three in the front and three in the back, and my job was to prepare the 120 economy meals in the galley. In those days the food came in large aluminum pans, vegetables separated from the meats, and you had to dish up every individual plate 120 times, six at a time, from the oven-heated pans. You had to make sure the food was cooked just right in every single pan, because those old-fashioned ovens could be very unreliable. And then there was the parsley, which had to be placed in a specific corner of the plate! We had cabin smocks in those days, which after take-off replaced the blouses while in flight, and these smocks used to be soiled and completely unpresent-

15

able after working the galley on one single flight. It was indeed a sloppy and hard job in there, and even if you were very organised, all that dishing up and maneuvering in this crowded area the size of a closet caused you to develop into a not so dignified stewardess. So much for the "Pan Am image." Reality turned out to be very much different from the superficial training. Here speed was of the essence. I managed to finish the service in about two hours. I had been in a frenzy, my head was spinning, and the purser told me I had done OK, but next time a little faster please!

This was a ten-hour flight, a strain on anybody but especially on a new-hire. I was so tired and had to learn so much, not just about service, but about the all-important safety procedures. How crowded it was on an airplane, no place to put anything, lines for the lavatories, no place to sit or stand, but in those days nobody ever complained. The airplanes were far less accommodating on space. There were no enclosed overhead bins, but everybody complied and only brought on board one little piece of hand luggage. Passengers got their food trays, there was no choice of meals, drinks were served from a hand tray, six at a time, pillows and blankets were overhead, and there were no extra amenities like headsets or hot towels, etc. That came much later.

For us, the flight attendants, there were just the jumpseats and a little semicircular lounge in first class to sit on for ten hours. I remember one of us made the remark that she was so exhausted, she did not care if the plane "landed in the ocean" (the Pacific in this case).

Other "particulars" in those days were the "triple-stacked" trays. Since we had more than one service on those long flights, the economy trays had to be doubled or tripled in the carriers (carts) due to the limited space. So we had to unstack them and organise them into individual trays, separating all of the little items, 120 times each. You can imagine how time-consuming!

The pursers, the ones who were in charge, in those days could be very demanding and disciplinarian. This German purser told me, after I had slightly burned some toasted sandwiches in the oven, "Turn them around!" in order to expose the mistake. Another one accused me of being lazy on a flight when I was feeling sick and had to sit down. The flights were eight to twelve hours long, and you did not always feel so good! Once I forgot to make coffee at the right time, and the purser was aghast—how could anyone be so careless! It became a federal case if you placed the parsley on the wrong spot on the plate, and that was in economy! We used to dish up every single plate for 120 passengers, six at a time, from big aluminum pans as well as scramble the eggs, which came half-cooked. No brown spots or green shades allowed! Once there was heavy turbulence, so the eggs hit the ceiling first and then landed as garbage on the floor. What did we do, after wiping up the mess? We got *raw* eggs from first class and scrambled from scratch! I can't remember how it was possible to have so many extra eggs in first class. The catering at that time was indeed generous. Maybe it was because in first class the eggs were made to order! Fried, sunny side up, poached, boiled, scrambled, sometimes for fifty passengers! Since the whole thing became impossible for one person to do in a galley the size of a closet and with very limited equipment, i.e., no frying pans or boiling pots or stove exactly (!), but just a tiny airplane oven, this insanity came to an end and it was eventually changed to scrambled or nothing.

There were no carts. All trays were hand-carried out

of the galley as well as drinks, six at a time on miniature trays.

The first-class service was a major, major production. Everyone who flew on Pan Am in those days remembers the china, the silver, the "clipper" menus, and the clipper plates with all different airplanes on them as gifts for the first-class passengers, the beluga caviar, the champagne, the wines, the lobster thermidor, the snow peas, the fabulous hors d'oeuvres, the fresh salad prepared on the plane, and especially the roast beef we cooked on board. We must have been the only airline in the world that had roast beef made on board! It took quite a bit of experience to work the first-class galley. No new-hire would be allowed to work it unless there were only two or three passengers to be served, and then under complete guidance and supervision by the purser. This was a cart-by-cart presentation starting with the "set-up" cart, consisting of the glasses and plates and silverware along with flowers and linens and folded napkins in all kinds of shapes. Then followed the caviar and hors d'oeuvre cart along with rolls and wines, then maybe a soup cart and salad tossed in the galley, then the entrées out of the galley at the same time as the roast beef cart with vegetables and potatoes and sauce. The roast beef was carved in front of the passenger, rare, medium rare, or well done. It was some trick to serve fifteen orders, all different, out of one single roast beef—you had to maneuver back and forth between the passengers so that 2A would get a rare piece and 5B would get it well done. After that came the cheese and fruit cart and finally the dessert cart along with liqueurs. On the Tokyo flights out of New York much later a total of seventy-three carts (two services) were served in the first-class cabin to thirty-six passengers (excluding eighteen more on the upper deck on the 747), which meant that as a flight attendant or as purser serving from the carts you had to ask passengers what they wanted in addition to describing the items 360 times during one single flight!

In those days anyway, in addition to "working like a horse" you had to look your best, unruffled, well groomed, polished—"looking like a woman" meant not only as attractive as possible, but looking like a lady and being one! We were ladies all right, with our white gloves and all.

"Thinking like a man" was something else, though. It could mean being "businesslike" in the performance of your job, which has always been a clever approach anyway. It also meant you were pretty much on your own, learned independence quickly both off and on the airplane, and learned to "tackle" every situation involving passenger problems or emergencies on board. Thinking like a man meant especially taking a certain distance from the scene, looking at it all completely objectively, not getting emotionally involved, and treating everybody alike. You did, of course, develop a certain toughness after a while, a savvy with people, an armour. This was necessary, in order to survive in this environment, with so many demands put upon you by the public, your colleagues, and especially the management. Finally, you were able to enjoy flying.

4

Flying the Pacific

Flying for Pan Am in the sixties was a great way of making a living, especially flying to the exotic destinations of the Pacific and the Far East. My first four years of flying based in San Francisco were probably the most exciting and rewarding. Flying was fun, an adventure. When you were called out on a trip, it was the destination that mattered: Tokyo, Hong Kong, Singapore, Bangkok, Djakarta, Hawaii, Tahiti, Fiji, Samoa, Sydney, Australia, and Darwin and Melbourne, New Zealand, and eventually the R and R flights in and out of Vietnam that took you to destinations like Saigon, Da Nang, Kam Rhan Bay, Taipei, Manila, and Guam. These were long flights, seven to ten hours, exhausting, but ever so worthwhile when you arrived, because the layovers could be anything from two to four days long. You were usually gone for at least ten days on a trip, sometimes twenty days. Often you were rerouted while away and could spend up to a month "on the line." Therefore, you developed good friendships and "home away from home" habits. The hotels became second homes, as well as the beaches, and the restaurants and the shopping areas and the swimming pools became areas of congregation.

Also, in those days during the heyday of flying the world, you were greeted at the hotels and the airports with a certain awe and respect, primarily because Pan Am had such a good name. From the moment we landed at an airport, our bags were carried for us through the terminal and into the hotel. If they did not exactly lay out the red carpet for us, they sometimes treated us to special parties and gifts of all kinds at Christmastime or if one of the crew members had a birthday. Because of the international date line in the Pacific, we often celebrated two birthdays, because the same day was repeated the next day!

Passengers were also happy to be flying. I don't remember anybody ever complaining about anything at all. I think they looked up to you as professionals much more than they do today. Although we were stereotyped then also, whatever the "sex image" role meant, we were still ladies to be reckoned with. When you walked in the aisle or in the airport, people looked up to you and were far more polite than today. Passengers enjoyed flying, just like we did.

In the Pacific we flew the Boeing 707 exclusively, with about 120 passengers in economy and sometimes up to 50 in first class! We were six stewardesses, three in the back and three in the front, and then we switched every leg. It was hard work, but since nobody ever complained, things went extraordinarily smooth. There were no special meals to speak of and not so many choices, but the food was better. There were no movies, no headsets, no on-board telephones of course, little reading material, no real amenities, and no entertainment (except us). You did have time to talk to people quite a lot. Passengers did ask you out on dates, of course, but only once in a while did you go. There were plenty of pilots around! And because we spent so much layover time with them, it was unavoidable that many romances developed. However, that was only in the Pacific and in the sixties, I am quick to point out. Most of the girls were in their twenties and, quite frankly, looking for a good time, and the pilots were for the most part divorced! Some of the married ones had sour relationships with their wives and generally drank too much. We had, as I have said, very long layovers in seductive places like Tahiti and Samoa, where the so-called "crew parties" flourished, and drinking and dancing and romancing and sex were all part of it. And it was great.

Tahiti

Jagged mountains, azure waters, lush emerald green vegetation, and black sand beaches—the most wonderful trip in the Pacific was unquestionably Tahiti. These French Polynesian islands consisted of the beautiful Mooréa and Bora Bora, amongst others. We had four-day layovers in Tahiti, i.e., Papeetee, from where we would take a little motorboat to Mooréa and spend all our time there. There was the famous "Bali Hai" hotel, set up by three American young men who bought the land from the French after a lot of maneuvering. They were Kelly, a lawyer, Muck, a salesman, and Jay, a stockbroker. The three have been featured in many magazine articles. They were all very different from one another, but they made up the perfect trio to run this romantic place made up of Tahitian huts as sleeping quarters, a great big outdoor dining room with long communal tables under a thatched roof, where everybody would help themselves to food from big pots of delicious fish and vegetables and fruit and wine and coconuts, and, finally, the most exciting entertainment in the evenings, consisting of us all dancing the Tahitian "Tamoure" the whole night long with the accompaniment of drums.

We were (the women) dressed in the *pareo,* which consisted of a bikini bra and a piece of cloth wrapped around the hips in exotic colors with a lei of flowers around the neck and the hibiscus flower behind the ear. Sometimes we even wore grass skirts. Since I love dancing, I had no problem with the quick hip movements to the drum, Tahitian style, which meant bending your knees and swaying to the left and right mostly on the forward part of your feet. People who did not bend their knees never got the knack of it; their fannies would stick out, so they were unable to move correctly. The Tamoure is a very sensual dance, quicker or slower than the "hula," depending on the drumbeat. After a number of "Rusty Nails" we would proceed in the middle of the night to a nightclub/hangout made famous by Marlon Brando, where we would continue dancing until morning. The floor there was made of clay, so your feet I remember were almost bleeding after all that grinding. By morning local people and some of us, too, were seen bent over on tables lying there immobile after, you guessed it, too much drink.

We still had a day or two to sober up before our flying. However, I tell you, in those days, especially out there in the Pacific, drinking and partying hard was an everyday activity on layovers, something that would be absolutely forbidden today and frowned upon by flight employees themselves. Today you may have a glass of wine (or two) with dinner in Rome, but in the sixties you drank all night. Nobody minded; it was just the way it was. The Federal Aviation Agency has since become much tougher on enforcing the eight-hour rule, meaning you cannot drink eight hours before a flight, after a lot of mishaps involving pilots' drinking. Some airlines are even stricter, requiring more than eight hours. The rule, of course, has always existed, however inadequate. You really need at least twelve hours of sobering up, wouldn't you say?

Hong Kong

Another wonderful destination was Hong Kong. I have no idea what it is like today, for I have not been there in twenty-five years, but in the late sixties, when we flew there, it was to me something out of a dream. I had a very good friend there who used to take care of our entertainment for two days in the form of nightclubs, the best Chinese restaurants, i.e., the best Chinese food I have ever had or trust I will ever have, and visits to his house in the mountains of the New Territories, which was something of a fantasy of many impressions, jokingly nicknamed "the Monastery." There were Chinese antiques, such as I had never before set eyes on, lacquer beds and porcelain cats and brocade draperies, all in black and burgundy and jade colors, and mysterious paintings, all a setting for smoking a pipe of opium or something. He had five dogs of various breeds and origins, one of which he called endearingly "the little whore." She was a very lovable fluffy-haired poodle and looked like "Blondie" in the comic strip. We had the most magnificent Chinese meals here also on top of the mountain in his garden, which was pleasantly overgrown and messy and infinitely charming. He worked in an antique store with some famous name and was very knowledgeable about everything in Hong Kong and took me and my friends to the best tailors to make our clothes as well as having boots and shoes made for very low cost even in those days, not to mention the jewelry stores, where we had bracelets practically made to order, rings redone, stones reset, and so forth. I bought a beautiful Australian opal ring there in 1967 for only $80.00.

Other Layovers

Another layover was Bangkok, with its floating market. We used to go to one single shop to buy Thai silk suits and dresses, one of the fashions of the sixties. Singapore and Djakarta were two other layovers we had but, unfortunately, were among the few where we only stayed twelve hours, so I do not recall very much. Pan Am had the round-the-world trips at that time, so we could just about circle the globe, or at least go halfway. Some Hawaii-based flight attendants actually flew all the way around the world. I don't know how many days they were gone.

And then there was Taipei, by far the most mysterious and spellbinding place I have ever visited. You feel there is both evil and good under the surface. Watching the Taiwanese dancers moving symbolically to the shrill, clangy music with their masked faces sent shivers down your spine. We used to stay in a hotel near the Imperial Palace; maybe it was a Hilton. One evening we were invited by the hotel management to have a "Mongolian barbecue" on top of a little hill opposite the palace under the most magnificent midnight blue sky I have ever experienced (except maybe in Africa). The sky was full of stars, and here we were "on top of the world," or so it felt, almost in total darkness except for the flames from the oast, where four kinds of meat were prepared and along with them fifteen (!) types of the most flavourful sauces, sesame, ginger and whatnot. The meats were placed in a sort of a bun and then the sauces spooned over. The taste of it all in the pure air of the night will forever remain one of my wonderful memories of flying in the Pacific.

Tokyo

For twenty years I flew to Tokyo, first out of San Francisco the first four years with Pan Am, and then I continued flying there for as long as I could out of New York until Pan Am sold the Pacific routes to United Air Lines, a sad day for me, sometime in the mideighties.

Yes, I loved Tokyo. It's because of the Japanese. They make me feel calm. They are discreet and show you respect in a most gentle way. In fact, I have never met a Japanese I didn't like (!), contrary to Germans, Italians, Americans, and Swedes! Sorry!

I flew to Tokyo in the sixties and the seventies and into the eighties, and it was always a treat. They tell me it is too expensive now, so I am happy I got the best of it in earlier times.

You used to arrive in the evening, a comfortable time, ready for bed. We stayed in the great hotels, ranging from the Prince Hotel to the Keio Plaza, twenty stories high, with dozens of various restaurants and shops and services from massage to beauty salon and shoe shine—you could live there for months, and some flight attendants did, being based there temporarily. It used to be a very desirable station to fly out of and thus a very "senior" position.

So, when you arrived in Tokyo, you either went out with some of the crew to have a bowl of delicious Japanese noodle soup (with dried green peas on the side!) and maybe hot sake along with it, or you stayed in your room, picked up the telephone, and asked for a massage. In about ten minutes a masseuse arrived; you could ask for her by name, depending how hard or soft a massage you needed. With very little dialogue, a few English words like "move over" or "back please," she proceeded to knead you in all the right places, especially along the spine, with "shiatsu" technique, and also your feet, which were always in agony after either a ten- or fourteen-hour flight, depending on where you had come from. For one hour these heavenly feelings lasted, and it cost maybe ten or twelve dollars.

Then you slept and slept and had breakfast the next morning, in your room maybe, consisting of banana slices with whipped cream, little cinnamon buns, and wonderful coffee, all served in dainty little chinaware with a rose on the tray. That is the other thing I liked about To-kyo—everything was rather small and dainty and pretty and tasty. After that, what I would do was have my hair cut in the hotel, and what a cut! They washed your hair and massaged your head from all sides, two of them at the same time, and then rinsed the hair and combed it wet over and over in the water. I have long and fine but heavy hair, so it is a lot of work. Then, after drying it, the stylist cut it with little snips in the most perfect way. After a visit there I always felt rejuvenated. In Europe and the States they rarely have time to pamper you in that way. It was pleasant as long as it lasted.

Then there was the shopping. It was the Oriental Bazaar, where everybody went, a store with beautiful bronze lamps, porcelain objects of all kinds, lacquerware, kimonos both modern and antique, screens and scrolls of endless varieties, cameras also, along with certain other household equipment like hairdryers, and so on. In addition to buying lamps and Japanese hibachis, this was the place where all the so-called "Tokyo bags" were sold. These bags were the most practical, all-purpose totes ever made—all sizes and in dark colors, so sturdy that we still have them many years later. I understand this shop went out of business when we stopped flying there.

The famous department stores were another experience. At the entrance as well as at the elevators were young women bowing, and when you bought an apple at the fruit stand, they wrapped it up in silky paper with string around it and a bow on top of it! There were so many employees everywhere, so they had time to give you magnificent service. They explained in detail all the features of an answering machine, for instance, and if something was not operating properly or was broken, they would repair it immediately and deliver it to the hotel at no charge.

In 1969 I bought a long strand of baroque pearls—it was so long that you could wind it twice around your neck—for only $90. A few years ago they were valued at over $2,000 or, in Sweden actually, $12,000 kronor.

When it came to dining in Tokyo, need I tell you about all the pleasures of Ski Yaki, Shabu Shabu, Korean barbecue, and on and on? Of course we visited places like Kamakura and the statue of Buddha there as well as little villages and offbeat marketplaces, but this is not a travelogue.

I would think the main reason for anybody to want a job as a flight attendant would be his or her love of travelling and seeing the world, or so it seems to me. We were thrilled to be flying, we wanted to see the world and learn all we could about it, go to as many places as possible, do all the shopping and sightseeing and partying and having exotic meals everywhere, a taste of it all! And we were never satisfied, we just wanted more of the world. We took extra trips on our time off even, down the Amazon River, safaris in Africa, trips to Seoul, Korea, and China, wherever we did not fly on our working trips. I don't see that kind of desire anymore. The new flight attendants view the job as just like any other. It's not their fault, far from it; they grew up under a different set of circumstances. However, the glamour is gone and gone forever. And I dare say it went out with Pan Am. You may think I exaggerate somewhat, especially about the "glamour," but only we who flew at that time know what I mean. Being a Pan Am flight attendant was something that could never, never be compared to anything else and can never be duplicated. It's history and we were part of it, and I'm so glad I was.

5

Vietnam—Flying the R and Rs

Part of flying in the Pacific were the Vietnam flights, the R and Rs. These were the "Rest and Recuperation" flights for the enlisted troops in and out of Vietnam to and from destinations like Saigon, Da Nang, and Cam Rhan Bay to Hawaii, Manila, the Philippines, Guam, and Taipei, Taiwan.

I was twenty-four years old when I flew those trips and did not quite realize that I was flying in and out of war zones and that the enemy were beneath us. I was so blasé and unaware that when the pilots were pointing to the ground indicating that there were the "VCs," I only shrugged my shoulders and asked, "What's that?" I knew, of course, that there was a war going on, but it never occurred to me that we ever were in any danger. Later I understood that Pan Am planes were actually shot at a few times. I also did not know that we were accompanied by air force planes, or maybe I just did not care to take notice. For me the Vietnam War was something that was being played out in the United States with all the demonstrations. In San Francisco, where I was based, all they talked about was the evil of the government. You were being bombarded with how useless and inane it all was and what a hero you were if you were a deserter, along with all the protest songs and flower children and peace

30

signs, and so forth. Now I had lived in Paris a few years earlier and listened to the exact same antigovernment rhetoric from my contemporaries in the French cafés about the French-Algerian war; therefore, all the American protesting by young people in the States was a mere repetition of what I had heard in Paris. So it never made much of an impression on me. I thought I had heard it all before. I was surrounded by all this negativism about the war, and I really think that influenced me in my attitude when I was flying those R and R trips.

Then, on one flight, I actually got a little awakening. The GIs on these flights were dog-tired, exhausted to the bone. Some of them would just sit there and twiddle their thumbs, unable to sleep. But there was one of them, what you would call a red-blooded American soldier, who suddenly spoke out, patriotically stating, "I'm proud to be in this war. I want to fight for my country no matter what!" At the time I thought it sounded refreshing.

As I have said, they were very tired always out of Vietnam, but that did not stop us from playing little jokes on them. In the sixties *Playboy* magazine was a big item, and sometimes we used to paste pictures of the Playboy bunnies onto the backflaps of the lifejackets, when we did the emergency demonstrations. When we turned around, in order to expose the backflap, plenty of cheers and catcalls followed.

We never had layovers in Vietnam, but one time I got the opportunity to see a little of Saigon. It was in the evening during a rather long transit stop. The crew was being asked to have dinner at the officers' club inside Saigon. We were driven through the streets accompanied by military escort, and what I mostly remember were the masses of sandbags stacked up against the walls of the little houses. Otherwise it was quite deserted, for obvious reasons. We had a good time at the club, interesting in a way, but nobody ever really talked about the war.

Vietnam was terribly hot, 100–130 degrees, and we had to wear our gloves and hats and girdles, remember! Then one day in Da Nang on another transit stop, we got a chance to take some of our clothing off under some rather comical circumstances. We were introduced to the so-called "Flying Tigers," a flying squadron out of that base. In their eagerness to get acquainted with us, "Western, round-eyed, blond women" they would give us a picture of a tiger in exchange for one piece of underwear from us. The sixties! We were only too happy to comply, so off came the girdles and the slips and the hose, and we got our pictures. However, we had not been informed that there was to be a "ceremony" along with it. This ceremony consisted of a kiss on your lips by one of the flyers. However, I sure was not prepared for what ensued. This man who kissed me in one big passionate move dipped me to the ground, while all his friends stood around us in a circle clapping and cheering. So there!

One of us six flight attendants—her name was Nancy; I will never forget her—wanted a little more. There was a very large painting of a tiger, and she could only have that one if she gave away all of her underwear. She did, and added her blouse, I think. Anyway, I remember her boarding the airplane in a raincoat (!) plucked out of her suitcase—we always had a lot of luggage with us, because we were gone so long on our trips. Although the uniform regulations in those days were very strict, as you can see, we still got around them.

By the way, some of us also wore wigs. Why? In order to hide our long hair, believe it or not. It was terribly hot, especially in this part of the world, and with the hat on top of it! The grooming regulations did not allow long hair at all, not even pulled back or up, but we refused to cut our hair. The only solution was wigs, which were not allowed either.

There was a story of a Swedish girl who had been photographed in Tahiti with her long hair flowing while playing a guitar. The Flight Service Office saw the picture and called her in and demanded that she cut her hair, whereupon she cried and cried and called in her mother, who also cried. They were finally let go, the girl's hair intact. Shortly thereafter, the grooming regulations were relaxed. Off came the wigs, as well as the girdles. Pantyhose had finally arrived on the scene.

I flew the R and Rs off and on for about two years, 1968–69, while Pan Am was the main civilian carrier there flying the troops back and forth until the famous last flight out in 1974, which was made part of a television feature later on, as we all know.

My memories from that time also include sad viewings of little old emaciated Vietnamese picking and rooting in the garbage bins left next to the plane to be picked up at the Tan Sun Nhut Airport in Saigon. We used to serve steaks on board to the soldiers, and there was always a lot left over.

One time I got the rather exhilarating opportunity to climb up in one of the F-4s. It was called the "Blue Max." The claustrophobic feeling of sitting there, one leg to one side and the other on the other side with all these instruments in the middle, cramped and crammed, ugh! When they landed, it was interesting to see the balloon behind them slow the plane down from such a tremendous speed.

I must also mention, finally, that we never had a choice of flying into Vietnam or not. We had to go; we could not refuse. It was part of the job or part of your seniority, rather, or lack of it. Consequently, we were issued the so-called "Geneva card," which entitled us to officer status, in case we ever became prisoners of war.

6

1970, Transfer to New York—Changing Altitude

I had not quite realized it, but the cozy, charming, and elitist atmosphere of flying the 707s with small crews and reasonably few passengers to faraway places with days of rich and eventful layovers was going to become more and more scarce. The 747 had arrived and with it crews of twelve to fourteen instead of five or six and passenger loads of 400 (!) instead of 150. I said I would never fly the 747—the 707s were still around, but it became increasingly more difficult to avoid progress.

I transferred to New York in the spring of 1970, a very significant move for me. I wanted to use my free time between flights for other activities. I felt I had enjoyed myself for four straight years but needed now to expand into other areas, and what better place than New York to do that? I never had any intention of quitting flying, however, because I knew that almost no occupation offered that kind of freedom and time off with a full salary. Apart from the crushing fatigue from jet lag, flying was like a part-time job. So the beauty of it was the opportunity you had to engage in other areas, be they studying or another part-time job or interest. However, most flight attendants at the time felt that flying was more than enough to handle and they needed all their time off to recuperate, and that was fine, too.

After settling down in the big city, I quite soon embarked upon activities like acting lessons (for ten months) and dancing lessons (jazz and modern), as well as cooking lessons (very inexpensive and worthwhile at the YWCA). I also started going around to the various modeling agencies, was sent on "go-sees" and "test-shooting" at photographers', acquired a model portfolio with all the pictures, and finally landed a variety of jobs ranging from some catalogue modeling, romance book covers, and lingerie print work to ads for medical supplies (!) and then later got some TV commercials, mostly modeling clothing and swimwear for department stores. I was able to join the Screen Actors' Guild finally and got minor film work, but plenty of it, which continued for years and years.

After arriving in New York I took an undergraduate course in philosophy at Hunter College for a whole semester, which proved to be a lot less fruitful than the other doings. What can you do with philosophy? Except maybe enjoy it—just. What I found rather surprising, though, was the relative lack of both discipline and interest among both students and teacher. The class was too large to make discussions about this subject meaningful, and the papers we wrote were all just about graded equally!

Except for the philosophy, it all turned out to be somewhat rewarding. I still do acting.

I also "checked out" as flight purser for Pan Am. So now I was flying the 747s. That meant that, as a purser, I had to be in charge on this large airplane, assign positions for the fourteen crew members, conduct briefings before every flight, which included safety and service procedures half an hour long, and be responsible for the well-being of 400 passengers. It was not so easy and smooth sailing anymore, because in the early seventies Pan Am started to have problems. Competition from other carriers began to erode Pan Am's market share. The management appeared to be wasteful and disorganized, and we were losing money. I remember one captain in a briefing mentioning that he thought "the end is near." There was suddenly so much paranoia and hysteria. However, Pan Am would still fly another twenty years. In the midseventies profits were made. The job was still great, and we still had a good name abroad. In the States we had few domestic flights, and the American public never seemed to grasp what Pan Am was all about. They flew on American, United, or Delta. Out of New York I was now flying to Europe, South America, Africa, the Middle East, the Far East, the USSR, and the Caribbean and Bermuda. It was a tremendous choice of flying.

The 747s became the mainstay of the fleet, but there were still some 707s around, which were used a lot on the charter flights. These flights were wonderful and quite adventuresome. I flew them quite a lot, to places like Warsaw and Venice. The layovers were rather unusual. In Venice we were taken from the airplane to the hotel in a gondola! When I stepped into it and saw the outline of that beautiful city, I thought I was dreaming. It looked theatrical, like I was approaching a stage. You would spend two or three days on layovers. Sometimes, though, when the crew arrived at the destination, there were neither transportation nor hotel rooms available, and that after eighteen-hour flights, so I, as purser, would spend much frustrating time trying to locate a Pan Am representative or make long-distance calls to Scheduling in New York. The pilots would have different flight patterns, so we were often stranded and on our own. The Warsaw charter flights were unforgettable. We had passengers who came right out of the fields on these flights and had never been near an airplane and really did not know how to behave on board. It was quite comical. When they were instructed how to fasten their seat belts, I remember one little man fastened the belt in the empty seat next to him. We had Saran Wrap around some of the meals, and instead of removing it, some of them would make a hole and eat the food through it. One passenger wanted to say something on the microphone but held it to his ear instead of his mouth! You can't expect people who do not live in a modern world to understand all technical things, especially on an airplane. In Saudi Arabia we had passengers boarding with live chickens and small trees!

Flying out of New York meant African destinations: Johannesburg, Nairobi and West Africa, namely Robertsfield. Because I had grown up in Africa, I did not want to fly there for some reason. Maybe I wanted to keep it as a fond memory not to be disturbed. However, twice I flew to Robertsfield, and what a time! Beautiful beaches—it was called Caesar's Beach—where almost everybody swam and sunbathed naked. The crew parties were notorious, much drinking, oh yes. There were good restaurants, and we were joined by employees of the Firestone Company, and there was much talk about the CIA being there, and so on.

India was another favorite spot for senior crews out of New York. I was in Delhi once and thought that everything looked prehistoric or biblical, especially on the way to the Taj Mahal. Everybody would buy snakeskin bags there, like they would buy carpets in Teheran, shoes in Rome, clothing in Paris, crystal in Warsaw, gold jewelery in Beirut, leather goods in Rio, and antiques in Buenos Aires.

South America was maybe the third most desirable

trip after India and Africa. Rio de Janeiro with its beaches, beauty and restaurants called the *churraskerias* along with the Camparinas, the local favourite cocktail. Buenos Aires, old and dignified-looking: old cars from the fifties, antique long portals into the buildings, somber hotel rooms with velvet curtains from ceiling to floor. In the early seventies you could have a magnificent dinner there with wine for a couple of dollars! And you were seated next to ladies with glittery dresses and fifties hairdos and garish makeup and old-world gentlemen making polite conversation, Glenn Miller playing softly in the background

People always ask, "What is your favorite place to fly to?" Well, it used to be Tahiti and then Hong Kong, but out of New York it became Tokyo, where I flew for the next twenty years.

7

Pan Am Starting to Slide

Deregulation had arrived.

Competition was threatening everywhere. Pan Am was losing money; a million a day, it was said.

The airplanes were starting to look a little time-worn—soiled carpeting, leaking galleys, lavatories in need of continuous repair, broken latches here and there, and we used to joke about how loose sidewall paneling or fixtures were being "taped" to hold in place. Maintenance items were written up in the logbooks over and over again never to be fixed properly, or when an overhaul was made, the problems still were not fully attended to. At least that was the way it was at JFK Airport. I think the airport facilities were largely to be blamed for the deterioration. As is well known, the trucking industry at JFK was controlled by the "Mob" directly or indirectly, and you would hear stories all the time about how Pan Am was being overcharged for many, many things. For instance, at one point we were told not to ask for extra catering items, because it would cost too much to pick them up with the trucks charging so much. "Don't even ask for an extra lemon; that would cost Pan Am fifteen dollars!"

There were rumours about catering never delivering extra soda cans or other things but still charging Pan Am for them. We were often short of catering items out of JFK and had to make do with what we had during the flight and then have to put up with passenger complaints. I remember one Tokyo flight, a Thanksgiving disaster. Instead of giving us two roasts of turkey, they only gave us one. This was a very prestigious flight with a full load of first-class passengers, and I had to give them all a sliver (!) of the turkey for Thanksgiving dinner. One passenger furiously stood up out of his seat, threw the napkin on the floor, and shouted, "Is this worth $7,000?" and then he would find fault with everything else on the flight as well, including me. It was my fault that the movie was not to his liking, that too many announcements were made, or there was not enough information, or something else. It was also my fault that he spilled brandy on himself and might get pneumonia (?!) after I removed the spots with soda water, a common practice we use on board to remove spills on clothing.

These kinds of trivial complaints were escalating in the seventies, as the image of Pan Am started to become somewhat tarnished. When an airline starts to lose money, the public somehow become more accusatory of the service, whether it is justified or not. On the other hand, when an airline is successful, passengers have much more patience with problems like delays for instance—one hour delay and very few complaints or none at all, whereas with an airline with financial difficulties a few minutes' delay and people start to grumble, "That's typical, always delayed, can't do anything right!" Unfortunately, that was what I very often heard from passengers in those days on Pan Am.

Another major adverse condition on board the airplane was the chronic understaffing. For some reason our management felt ten to twelve crew members on the 747 were perfectly enough to take care of 400–500 passengers, whereas on the other major airlines of the world fourteen to eighteen was the norm. No wonder, then, that we received our share of passenger complaints. Along with Eastern and TWA, we were on the bottom half of the list. Yet we had the most magnificent first-class service, maybe the best in the sky, and we did it with just three of us on the 747, when other airlines had fewer first-class passengers, a smaller cabin than we had, and more flight attendants. However, in the economy cabin the call buttons would always be ringing, while the five or six overworked and harassed flight attendants were trying just to get the service to progress, and there were three hundred to four hundred passengers depending on the configuration.

The Tokyo flights were almost worse—there were only three of us (!) for *100* business-class passengers with all their special requests. On a Paris flight a letter came from a passenger in our clipper-class section (that was Pan Am's business class) bemoaning the fact that we were "grotesquely understaffed," but that we had acquired along with it "an air of resignation" and that you had to have "the patience of God" to be a flight attendant.

When we complained to management year after year, there was always resistance and excuses. At one company meeting, I remember when we were talking about passengers waiting and waiting for service and could we increase the staffing with at least one more flight attendant, the answer was a shocking, "That is only from your point of view!" The passengers' point of view apparently did not enter into it.

Another time on a Tokyo flight a flight attendant working alone (!) on the upper deck with eighteen first-class passengers voiced her upset to one special Pan Am vice president, who told her she "could be replaced." I have to say, though, that was one of the worst scenarios I ever heard of. We worked very hard but with a certain gusto, and I don't think management was ever quite aware of the real situation on the airplanes. They sat there in first class and savored all the goodies and did not care to look behind them. That was certainly the case with certain executives who later in the eighties referred to the economy passengers as the "riffraff." So much for taking care of the passenger.

So, I think Pan Am had itself to blame for a lot of its woes. It was not just competition and deregulation. The management was arrogant, and no one was really in charge seemingly. Since Juan Trippe, the founder of Pan Am and the inventor of the glory of Pan Am, the ensuing CEOs were too autocratic or too isolated or surrounded by yes-men too much or out of touch with the employees, resulting in constant union battles, so that the rift between management and labour grew wider. Maybe there were many people who really tried to improve on things, but when there is little communication between workers and managers, starting with the top, and that is the key, then mistrust builds up and the "blame game" is in full swing. And that was the one thing that always would irritate me—being blamed for management's mistakes (more of that in the chapter "The Smile").

Our union struggles with management were many throughout the years. We would have a contract, and they would violate some of the rules over and over again. We would take pay cuts over the years, so-called "cutbacks" in our working conditions, and an endless stream of give-backs in exchange for really nothing. In my opinion, the worst of it all was the pension freeze for all of us by Mr. Acker in 1984. I cannot understand how it could be legal. Instead of getting around 60 percent of your pay at retirement, you would end up with only 10 percent, doled out

43

from the Pension Benefit Guarantee Corporation. This amount had become a paltry few hundred dollars for most of us, and that was after flying for Pan Am twenty or thirty years. Not so for the CEOs and all the vice presidents, who got away with millions after only sitting on the board for a number of years. Perfectly legal!

In spite of all my carping here, believe it or not, I would not trade my life with Pan Am and all those years for anything in this whole world! It was worth it all the way, because we had the fun and the adventure and the learning that only go with flying for the "World's Most Experienced Airline." You may snicker at that ad slogan, but it was true as long as it lasted.

8

The Smile

Hold that smile for fifteen hours and do it sincerely!
                              —from a union letter

There is a book called *The Managed Heart,* by Dr. Arlie Russell Hochschild, that examines the emotional labour done by flight attendants. This is curious labour indeed, she says, a labour that has been generally ignored by both employer and employee. She feels that flight attendants are diplomats representing companies instead of countries. The flight attendant's entire appearance sends a message. A flight attendant is treated as a representative of the company, for better or for worse. If the company has made some mistakes along the way—some luggage was lost; the overhead light does not work; a connection has been missed; there has been an hour delay; the seat is too tight; the meal is cold—then the flight attendant is held responsible for all the disasters. When you are treated that way, there are various ways to react. One way is to say, "Yes, I am the company and I'm proud of it"—in which case the flight attendant takes the anger personally. Or the flight attendant can say, "I am being treated as if I were the company, but I'm going to move left and let the arrow hit the window. I'm responsible for doing my job. I'm not responsible for luggage I did not lose." You have to adjust yourself so that you don't get your feelings all torn up.

45

Emotional labour is the work it takes to feel the right feeling for the job. With the growing service industry, more of us have jobs face-to-face and voice-to-voice with the public. We are not an assembly line bending metal with blow torches, a situation in which you do not have to love the metal; you just have to bend it. The flight attendant's work is dealing with an assembly line of people, and the job is to forge relationships, even if they are just five minutes long. Doing this is not a matter of flexing your muscles, but rather your feelings. You can't form a relationship without feelings.

Emotional labour is a kind of human gift that we can give each other if we choose to. Public life very much depends on it. It becomes a problem when management starts to manage how we make emotional exchanges and puts us into a "speed-up" situation—when we are forced to give out emotion under circumstances we cannot control. That leads workers to pay a psychological cost that has not been named or understood.

When Dr. Hochschild interviewed a lot of flight attendants, she found that most of them enjoyed their job not only because of the travelling, but because it also had its intrinsic rewards. However, there was a lot of talk about stress. People were not talking about it as a "fun" job. The flight attendants would say, "Don't get me wrong—I don't want another job; I like this job." But somehow as they talked over the various aspects of the job, stress was mentioned repeatedly. The majority of the work was pleasant enough, but portions of the time were psychologically taxing. This is important.

The new flight attendants, the ones out of training, can be very vulnerable to burnout unless they learn how to act, how to "depersonalise" or "personalise" their relationships to the passenger, and how to attune to the situation aboard the aircraft When this happens, the job can be a lot of fun and stress can be avoided. But then, even if a flight attendant learns how to act well, there is another problem. Is the act part the "company me" or the "real me?" What happens when you come home? At a party you may wonder, *Is this just a personality I have put on for the party?*, then decide *Yes maybe it is, but it is still me.* Or, *Yes, it's not the real me,* or *maybe I'm not sure who it is. . . .* When a company asks you to present a persona, it is as if you are the company persona. The ownership of the persona is in question now. Is it for rent? Is it completely you? It's ambiguous. The company and the person are the same?

According to management, what attitude should we have? Smile, smile, smile, and smile some more!

Dr. Hochschild answers:

Oh my. My initial response is, "Have you ever tried doing that for fifteen hours? I wonder if the company itself realises the emotional labor that is behind smiles.

If the company is going to ask workers not just to smile but to smile sincerely—then the burden is on the company to make working conditions such that a pleasant disposition does come naturally, in which case there should not be a speed-up, but a reasonable workload, reasonable layovers. It's not just a matter of wages; it is a matter of working conditions, which would make the smiling disposition easier to come by. Part of creating this atmosphere is to put into employees' hands some control over the working conditions. A happy worker is one who feels not only that working conditions are good, but that he or she can have a say; he or she can affect working conditions. That is the way you get sincere smiles!

Because of the price wars and deregulation, compa-

47

nies are ever more fiercely competing with each other not only at the level of ticket prices, but also in the notion of sincere service. And so companies are, in fact, putting a harder press on flight attendants to be nice and smile and smile some more.

On the other hand, working conditions are deteriorating. The pressure to smile increases while, because of working conditions, the reasons to decrease. It is a contradiction. And so people say, "Flight attendants aren't as friendly as they used to be. They are angry, surly . . . why would you write a book about them?" And Dr. Hochschild responds: "It is a response to the deterioration of working conditions."

Getting credit for emotional labour is incredibly important. We want stress to be acknowledged at the bargaining table with management. Dr. Hochschild also says that with the increased presence of male flight attendants, the "coffee, tea, or me" perception is waning. It was good for business but hard on women. The image says: "I am cute, but I am dumb. I am also consumable; I'm for sale." Most flight attendants do not want to carry a chip on their shoulders, but they sure get offended when an ad-drenched male passenger says, "Give me my smile," as if he had bought it. This is degrading. That is why you need self-esteem to be nice. Anyway, that was emotional labour.

The way it was

Graduation, May, 1966

On the beach in Tahiti

Relaxing in Bali Hai, Tahiti

In the cabin during the '60's dressed in smocks and wigs

In transit in Saigon

On board the F-4C in Danang

The troops disembark from R&R in Saigon

Eva Engström with a Vietnamese orphan

Uniform changes from the '60's to the '80's

"The Professor"

Lunching in São Paulo

Reading on the jumpseat on an R&R flight

Liv Andersen and me in the first-class cabin

Crew on the way to the lay-over hotel

Troops returning from Desert Storm

On the runway before leaving North Carolina; Britt Marie with co-worker. Desert Storm

Playing the accused mother in *Presumed Innocent*

Cigarette girls in the Copacabana scene of *Raging Bull*

Playing a hooker in *See No Evil, Hear No Evil*

A friend and me in *Cocktail*

Moonlighting model shots from the '70's

AIMÉE BRATT

In the briefing office

Susan Aragona with Supervisor

My last flight, San Francisco-New York

9

Murphy's Law—A Hellish Charter Flight

Some flights were indeed out of hell! This is an excerpt from a report made by the senior purser of this flight to the company. I was the junior purser:

Dear Ms. Smith,

(1)

While boarding in Lisbon several passengers were given seats in the first-class section by our ground staff. When other passengers saw this, they continually bombarded Flight Service complaining of numerous physical disorders such as fear of flying, cancer, pacemaker, swollen parts and pieces of every description, etc. No less than a hundred passengers had a problem which required a first-class seat. No requests beyond those assigned in Lisbon were honored. Several passengers threatened action of various sorts against the crew, especially myself.

A full hot tray service was provisioned. Since there were forty short, crew meals were served to passengers, which resulted in another twenty-two meals missing. I requested that the engineer radio ahead for the additional meals. However, we were told that commissary requests of any kind could not be handled due to a strike by that department.

With only one hour and a half to Frankfurt it was nearly impossible to serve and cook 370 meals, serve drinks, coffee, tea, etc. especially under these conditions.

(4)

This particular entree is almost impossible to unwrap.

(5)

All four coffeemakers in the main galley were inoperative.

(6)

A major water leak in galley 1C, which flooded the first four rows behind that galley. The crew now had to deal with thirty cold, soaking wet, angry tourists.

(7)

All of zone ABC had no audio. The music lovers were outraged.

(8)

All of zone HJK reading lights were either turning off or on. The sleepers fought it out with the readers. The crew of course lost.

(9)

Several non-smokers were in the smoking section and added themselves to the first class seat demanders to correct the problem. All had severe asthma, lung problems, etc.

(10)

After thirty minutes on the ground in Frankfurt I became aware that the commissary loading had not begun. After many inquiries it became evident that we were not going to be provisioned at all. It turned out that Frankfurt thought Lisbon was to provide the meals and Lisbon thought Frankfurt would. The meals were really in Shannon, but we were not going there!

(11)

After one hour on the ground it was discovered, with the passengers still on board, that due to the shortstaffing it would be three hours before any commissary could be started. It was decided to groundfeed the passengers in Frankfurt, but the news came that the restaurant was closed for reconstruction. This was becoming a long duty day, close to seventeen hours,* so I assembled the crew, and five of them wanted to cancel out, which would mean hotel space for all the passengers. By this time the passengers were getting out of hand, and the crew was breaking down under the abuse. There was only one more option, and that was to go without meals. A vote was taken, and in fifteen minutes we were airborne, no commissary at all and a crew driven to mutiny or murder.

It must be noted that every crew member did an outstanding job given the conditions of this mess. I hope they are each sent a commendation for continuing to defend our airline in the face of this flight, and especially Ms. Bratt, the other purser, who took constant abuse from passengers for the entire fourteen hours. I sincerely hope this will be remembered when the trivial complaints from the passengers commence to arrive concerning my crew and myself, as a result of this nightmare flight.

The Purser

---

*Seventeen hours was the maximum duty day according to our contract. There were no FAA rules in regards to duty time at that time, which has since changed.

10

An Airplane—Not the Ritz!

No indeed. An airplane is not the Ritz; it is just this piece of aluminum flying in the sky, and it has its limitations.

"What do you think? This is not the Ritz, you know!"

These were offhand comments made describing the way it was on the Pan Am 747s in the seventies and the eighties. However, the first-class food had originally been catered by Maxim's of Paris. People would come on board and expect a restaurant.

No, there were 400–450 seats on the big 747 aircraft, out of which 30–50 could be first class and 50–100 were clipper class (business), depending on the configuration, which changed according to routes. There were usually four galleys, one on the upper deck, which was either first class or clipper class. There was no piano bar, which was sometimes believed, or lounge, where people could congregate. One galley was downstairs for first class, another one in clipper and economy combined, and one other large galley in the back of the plane for economy class.

For serving that many passengers, the galleys were very small. It was certainly no "kitchen," the galley. There was no refrigerator or microwave oven (!), as some people believed. There was minimal counterspace not really designed for working on, it was merely an extension of the oven space or a top on top of the cart stowages. You could not afford to make mistakes, because there was no room to manoeuvre. Whoever designed those galleys should have tried working in them, we used to say.

During the service there were five or eight flight attendants moving around in an area of about five to eight feet, and that was the big galley. Ideally you would have been comfortable with two or three people in there.

There were hundreds of trays and meals to be handled in this area. Add to that drawers of ice, boxes of soft drinks, liquor kits, wine coolers, and a lot of serving carts that were secured to the floor in their spaces. If you moved one out, it took up half the space in the galley, so you can imagine how organised one had to be.

We moved past each other like snakes, bending and reaching over one another in a continuous ritual. A regular housewife could not have stood it for long. The average person would also have been overwhelmed by the myriads of demands during the heat of the service coming from all corners of the big plane. The 747 was so large that an awful lot of walking back and forth in the aisles was unavoidable. The reason that passengers saw the flight attendants doing that so much was because the serving equipment was in different places all over the airplane! If I needed a fork (!) and I could not find it in one galley, I had to walk through the entire length of the aisle to the other galley. Insanely impractical? Yes, of course. It was an airplane! Not a restaurant! It was crowded, the equipment was stowed all over the place, and there were hundreds of safety rules to be adhered to.

Charter flights were especially crowded. While passing out trays, you were slowed down by extra demands on your way back to the galley. The serving carts did stream-line the service to a certain degree, but some flights were still not as "smooth" as others, often because of a large amount of "special meals" to be delivered. It could get out of hand, since Pan Am for a while advertised special "menus" with a variety of exotic names. You needed an extra flight attendant just to take care of these "extras," and we were understaffed already. Religious or dietetic meals, of course, were always justifiable.

Also, Pan Am had a fondness for offering three choices of meals in the economy class, when two would have been enough. It slowed down the service tremendously. You would run out of one item, passengers would be angry, there would be "food arguments" over such trivia, and a negative "snowball" effect was created; the service could practically fall apart. You can imagine asking three hundred to four hundred passengers if they prefer chicken, fish, or lasagna, every single one of them, how time-consuming! One or two entrées of good quality should have been served. But for Pan Am, who was penny-wise and pound-foolish, this was the cheaper way.

Sometimes the trays were "bulkloaded," and we had to set everything up from scratch, another unnecessary and time-consuming job, usually resulting in passenger complaints because of all the waiting. If you were the "galley person," it was a hard job to organise the galley, which meant repositioning service items for better access, preparing things on the ground (usually during the boarding process) to be ready "to go," and sometimes redoing the whole job that catering had done, which was often impractically or unworkably loaded for us. So-called "uplifts" would arrive at the last minute, if the passenger count went up, and the commissary, who had little time, would just place everything on the galley counters. Now you had to find a space for these "late arrivals" in the already-overstuffed galley.

Suppose you did not have a special vegetarian meal

on board. Instead of trying to tell the passenger there was none on board, you went to first class and got a plate of vegetables and hoped that would settle it. It usually did. However, you could spend twenty minutes of serving time (now the rest of the crew was even more understaffed) explaining, solving, and apologizing. The airplane was not a restaurant or a bar or a hotel. When we ran out of caviar, that was it.

In those days also for some reason (I don't see it today anymore) people would stand around drinking in the aisle, partying and smoking. This was obviously a safety hazard. If the airplane hit turbulence, a cigarette could be dropped and a fire could start, especially if it fell in an area where it would be impossible to retrieve, i.e., behind the fuselage.

Even though the lavatories had automatic fire extinguishers and smoke alarms, fires did happen in there. On one particular flight from Italy it happened in the middle of the night. It was a full flight, and someone in the nonsmoking section had wanted a cigarette. There were no seats in the smoking section, so he lit up in the lavatory. The smoke alarm went off, but not until the entire area was engulfed in smoke from the discarded cigarette butt—in the trashcan! It took four flight attendants and three extinguishers to control the smoke and calm the passengers and relocate them temporarily. In the waste chute were five or six cigarette butts already from former flights. Smoking was to be done at your seat, sitting down, but these safety rules were consistently ignored—at that time.

11

Passengers—A Sample of the World in the Cabin

The Pan Am passengers were people who wanted to go from point A to point B with a minimum of obstacles and worry. They had a goal in mind, whether it was pleasure or business. They paid a reasonable price and expected acceptably good service. They had a certain amount of patience, understanding weather delays, why airplanes had to wait on the runway (even if the captain did not always make an announcement), and why there were security checkpoints at the airports, being fully aware of the terrorist threats all over the world, having read about the tragic attacks during the last twenty years. They also understood that airlines had been losing a lot of money lately due to fare wars, fuel crises, cutthroat competition as well as foolish management decisions and therefore did not challenge the airline employees unnecessarily when things did not go so smoothly. The passengers complained from time to time but generally used common courtesy and common sense. Thank heavens for those passengers, the majority, because if they had behaved like the minority, about which I am going to tell a few tales, the airlines would not be in business.

There was this minority who never used common courtesy or common sense. These were the people who committed "cabin crimes": creating scenes during boarding because they were "promised an aisle seat" but could not get it in the last minute because of a full flight; or behaving like children if there was, for instance, no mustard on board for their snack sandwich, or running to the bathroom two minutes before touchdown, when the nonsmoking sign had lit up, just to "freshen up," or ignoring the safety signs at any time (during turbulence) or getting so inebriated that shouting matches or even fistfights erupted.

These things happen today also of course, but I think to a somewhat lesser degree because of changes in the industry. However, on Pan Am, especially in the seventies and the eighties, they occurred quite frequently. As I have said, it had something to do with Pan Am's financial situation. We were always being blamed for the most trivial reasons. It was also Pan Am's fault. Passengers would be boarding, already surly and irritable, especially at JFK Airport, because, quite honestly, the ground handling there left plenty to be desired—some of our ground staff were well known for their discourtesy. During flight most passengers just sat there and tried to enjoy it, got a little sleep, read a book, or talked to someone next to them. They accepted the fact that the quarters were a little cramped, lavatories were small, galley areas were too busy to stand around in, and there were smoking and nonsmoking sections. They showed consideration, especially if the flight was full. It was crowded, and they understood that it would not be as comfortable as promised in the advertising pictures.

That was obvious, you may think, but at the time there were actually people who did think that the flight was especially made up for them, that they were going to be wined and dined like in the pictures, and that anything they asked for would be taken care of immediately, like, for example, demanding four seats for yourself.

The Egotist

He had a comfortable seat in first class and did not ask but demanded to stretch out in economy over four seats, thus limiting the space for the economy passengers in that area, who also may have wanted to stretch out a little. He lay down there without taking care to ask if anyone was occupying the seats. Well, there was one, in the lavatory, whose seat was one of the four. When that passenger came back, a heated argument followed. I was called. The first-class passenger insisted he had a "right" to stay there; he "always" got four seats in economy to sleep on. I could not reason with him and called the captain. The first officer came down and tried to persuade him to move back to first class. That did not work either. Finally, the economy passenger moved to another seat in disgust or for the sake of peace.

The Sarcastic

Some Europeans could not help making comments that they only interpreted as witty but were actually quite offensive. This was years ago, when different nationalities were more marked than today.

Something was not pleasing to this particular British passenger, so he commented, "What can one expect from an American airline, hu, hu!" or "Is Pan Am getting primitive .. !"

At the time also, even Americans would consider it

"chic" to criticize their own, so you would hear comments like, "That's what you get from Pan Am; Air France would never . . . !" I used to answer, "I never heard the French put down their airline." (Air France was noted for their snobbish crews and indifferent service.) When the Americans heard my European accent, they would squirm a little.

The Insecure

These people were very difficult to deal with, because no matter how you presented yourself, they would interpret your behaviour as a putdown. I am talking about certain passengers who may have been "upgraded" to first class and now felt that they had to "show off." You served them wines and cheeses or desserts they had never heard of. There was this man who wanted to appear worldly, so he asked to see all the wines and taste them and then said something like, "Is this all you have?" and on Pan Am we of course had excellent wines and champagnes. I hid my true feelings and served him his Coke with the sole amandine! These situations could be time-consuming and disrupted the service flow in view of the fact that at Pan Am we were understaffed. Other passengers would be waiting, I was often alone in the cabin, and this passenger had to monopolise me with this trivia about wines, which he knew nothing about anyway.

Some Insecures would make comments like, "I usually go first class, but today I have to sit back here, because my secretary made a mistake . . . ," as if something were tainted about the economy class or they felt the need to impress me. Diplomats and celebrities often sat in economy. First class was prohibitively expensive. Few people really paid for it. It usually filled up with "upgrades." Some people felt "slighted" for not sitting there and became outright hostile. I will never forget this well-dressed German gentleman, or so I thought he was at first, who came up from clipper class gesticulating and shouted into first class, "This is sick, sick, sick!" When I asked what was the matter, he got even more agitated. "First class is sick. . . . Everybody should be sitting there!"

Then there were the abusive others, usually men, who took pleasure out of harassing the stewardesses: "Why don't you smile for me!" when they were pushing heavy carts in turbulence. Or they would drive you crazy with impossible demands on purpose. One man rang the call button very often and asked for little nothings like turning off his reading light or another drink after one had already been served. This type of passenger was craving attention and ego massaging, but we had no time for that in Pan Am.

Then there was the inconsiderate lot: parent passengers who did not mind that their children were misbehaving, ringing the call button a hundred times and asking for Cokes for no other reason but boredom. These parents also did not mind that their noisy brats ran around all over the airplane disturbing other passengers or, worse, were dangerously in the way when we were coming with our serving carts in the aisles. They thought their kids were cute.

And the restless, who wanted to be entertained: They would be in your way, taking up valuable galley space even during the service, blocking the aisles, restless, demanding, unsatisfied. You would politely ask them to move to the side, and they would glare at you. What if I spread myself all over their desks, hindering their work? And I would not be as charming as their cats.

In those days *women* passengers were never a problem. They were understanding and patient and seldom made a fuss. They also seemed to enjoy themselves on board more than their male counterparts. They were more relaxed. Unfortunately, later on, as the years went by and along with the women's movement, stewardesses were criticized in women's magazines and sometimes by "career women" for "catering only to men." We were told that we did not give other women the same service or attention as we did the men. I felt that it was an unfair evaluation of the situation in light of the workload we had on the airplane. To us, all passengers were the same, and there really was no time for sexist behaviour, especially since we ourselves were women also travelling alone, staying in hotels, and so on. On international flights, which were the bulk of Pan Am's routes, we were handling passengers of all nationalities along with their cultural differences, women and men, black and white and yellow, so one had to be very flexible indeed, "catering" to their different types of needs. The mere thought of "women passengers" not being treated equally to men passengers was a bit frivolous, I think, as well as a little insulting to us, and definitely this criticism undermined our profession. Today, I think, flight attendants are viewed a little more neutrally, and the sexism is becoming obsolete.

Then we had the arrogant passenger, who did not think it was necessary to say "thank you" or "please" or would mutter something unintelligible when addressed. He would come on board with a huge suitcase or suitbag and expect butler service. A 115-pound flight attendant struggled to make it fit into a cramped closet but could hardly lift it or carry it. This passenger, maybe double her weight, would neither thank her nor offer any help. As a purser at Pan Am I would tell my crew not to do those kinds of services but show the passenger how to stow the bag himself. Obviously, we would help mothers with children, older ladies, and other people who really needed assistance with settling in the cabin. However, I know of more than one flight attendant who, in her eagerness to help, developed slipped discs and arm and shoulder injuries and chronic back problems she still has today.

We had our share of the funny passengers. They came from all over the world and had never been on an airplane before.

On a charter flight out of Eastern Europe once we carried some people who had only grown up in the fields and were completely unfamiliar with airplanes and therefore did some extraordinary things on board. Sometimes we had really primitive people on board, who had never seen toilets or bathrooms. In the remote areas of the world we flew, an "accident" in the passenger seat or in the aisle of the cabin would happen from time to time.

Also in the Middle East, on our flights to Mecca, the so-called Hadj flights, as well as to other destinations, they would bring live chickens on board. On a flight to Baghdad once, one man sat down in the aisle and tried to start a little fire for cooking.

There were also the animal passengers, and I am not talking about the dogs and cats in the "belly." Live snakes were found in the cabin that escaped from the cargo compartment. And how about the rat who flew thousands and thousands of miles without paying a cent? The frequent flyer program had not been introduced then.

Today, passengers of different nationalities behave more or less the same on board an airplane, but during the sixties and seventies and into the eighties every country had a national airline and kept it so, so the boundaries were far more marked. There were no mergers (just a few) or takeovers or code-share partners like lately. The French passengers on board Pan Am would behave as if everybody spoke their language. They only spoke French, and they, more or less correctly, assumed that since you were a stewardess, you spoke their language. However, if you did not speak it very fluently, they would answer you back in rather poor English. They also detested Coca-Cola.

The Scandinavians always drank a lot but in my view *were* the most polite and considerate of all passengers worldwide. I am not saying that because I am Swedish. It was a cultural difference.

The Spanish-speaking people from Central America, South America, and Puerto Rico were all different of course, but there was certainly something that could be described as "latino" behaviour. This hissing sound in the cabin, "pssst!," was a shock at first, but when you gave them your attention, they smiled and joked and were warm and sweet.

The Japanese were always my favourite passengers. I flew Tokyo trips for twenty years, and *never* (it is really true) did a Japanese passenger complain on my flights. If they were displeased about something, they would always ask very politely if it could be changed. They were totally civilised, gentle, and patient. Those were hard, long flights out of New York, fourteen hours nonstop, and as I have mentioned, we were chronically understaffed. Passengers often did not get adequate service as a result thereof, especially in clipper class, all 100 of them with only three flight attendants working there, but never did I hear a negative word out of Japanese passengers. They could clearly see how we were struggling to get the service done, so what was the point of complaining?

Some of the American passengers on those flights made up for it instead, aggravating the situation. American passengers may have been within their rights to be angry, though, paying the fare for such a long flight and receiving this understaffed service, but it did not serve any useful purpose to have a temper tantrum and place the food tray on the floor in the aisle and ring the call button and yell expletives. That did not help matters at all. Now we had to deal with one more difficult situation instead, which exacerbated the already-burdensome procedures we were faced with.

Yes, American passengers always wanted "value" for their money. It was not enough to get transportation for the fare they had paid. They wanted good service and all the "extras"—choices in food, extra legroom, extra closet space, extra individual attention, fast baggage handling, fast check-in, fast everything, and they were often frustrated when they arrived in foreign countries, where local customs and procedures were slower. They were often an impatient lot. In all fairness to them, things always did run more smoothly in the United States. They were used to that. Why pay more? Competition is a good thing, or so we thought, until we ran into airline deregulation.

12

Passenger Stories

"What is the time here?" asked an unsuspecting woman passenger at 31,000 feet. She was not interested in the local time in New York, which we had just left, or in London, to where we were flying but the exact spot over the ocean, thinking the time "moved" with the flight. She had obviously never heard of time zones.

There was a lady with a towel over her arm: "Where can I take a shower?"

An American southerner arriving from the Middle East and Europe was being served coffee on our plane. She asked in her southern drawl, "Is this American coffee?"

"Oh yes," said the stewardess.

"That's just wonderful, 'cause I'm sick and tired of that *muuud!!*"

We were coming through with the beverage cart, on it anything from champagne to Coke and everything else for the passenger to see. When a stewardess asked the passenger what he wanted to drink, the answer was: "What do you have?"

Another one: "Would you like coffee or tea?" Answer: "Yes, please!" And: "Where is the ladies' room?"

On a short flight a male passenger was asked several times what he wanted to drink. He shook his head; he wanted nothing. When the NO SMOKING sign came on for landing, he wanted to know what kind of white wine we had!

A passenger from India demanded the following from the stewardess: "Change the bebe; change the bebe!"

"Into what?!" was the surprised reply.

Another one from the same country wanted a drink of water. Since he had already asked for water several times, the stewardess suggested he use the fountain outside the lavatory whenever he got thirsty again. He exclaimed, "Madam, madam, I don't drink toilet water!"

A disappointed male passenger said to a male flight attendant, "Where is the leg?!"

He answered, "Here, I've got two legs."

Some passengers tried to be very savvy about our nationalities. They would ask me if I was Hungarian or Icelandic!

One of us was asked once if she was German, because in his view she behaved a little brusquely. She was a rather gentle Danish girl, so she said, "No, I'm Danish, and what do you know about Germany anyway?" She felt he was rather biased.

Some comments were outright sexist: One passenger remarked, "You, a *female* purser!" Often passengers would address a male flight attendant, assuming he was the one in charge, when I was standing next to him, my PURSER sign clearly visible on my jacket. In Latin countries they still do.

There was this passenger who could not believe that Pan Am had "female pursers" first of all, and then this little fat man sneaked into the first-class galley when we did not notice and ate all the blueberry muffins reserved for first-class breakfast!

And other things they did! This lady from the economy section stalked right into first class and proceeded to pick up and eat the fruit from one of the set-up carts. When she was asked to leave, she could not understand why: "What's the big deal? I thought I could have a banana!"

"Do you eat, too?" asked a passenger, seeing the flight attendant on her jumpseat. He was standing right over her, unaware of the need for privacy that most people have when consuming a meal. Annoyed, the flight attendant offered him a biteful jokingly, hoping he would get the hint and move away. Instead, lo and behold, he to her amazement, accepted a taste!

One passenger refused orange juice, changed his mind several times, and finally wanted it, looked at his eggs in contempt and did not want them, and then changed his mind again. After that he suddenly yelled, "Someone take my tray away!"

Passengers would quite often ask the question: "Do you turn around now and go right back?" after a seven-hour night flight across the Atlantic.

We did not sleep; we did not eat. We were "fixtures" of the airplane, not quite human, some kind of robots in uniform. People had strange perceptions of us indeed.

When I was little, I believed that stewardesses ate and slept on the plane and that they had wardrobes on board with beautiful dresses, because they always looked so glamorous on the layovers, But that was a long, long time ago.

In first class during the sixties people would come on board nicely dressed in suits and white gloves on their way to Paris. That changed during the deregulation times in the seventies. You started seeing passengers boarding in dirty jeans and sneakers and putting their feet up on the seats in front of them and, along with that, abominable manners. In the sixties people were civil, whereas years later passengers would use foul language all over the airplane. One woman passenger in first class, I remember, was so rude. She wanted the remaining items on the table to be taken away. We told her there was still dessert coming, and in Pan Am it was, as we know, a beautiful cart-by-cart presentation. She told a male flight attendant, "Tell the stewardess . . . that I'm finished when I'm finished!" and, "Leave that [a water glass] for Christ's sake!"

The following are a few examples of passenger stories, that range from the peculiar to the idiosyncratic to the obscene.

A lady in first class was served caviar. She did not know what it was, so it was explained to her that it was fish roe. "Oh," she said. "You mean fish eggs . . . could I have them scrambled?"

Another first-class passenger was served danish in the morning. They were rather sticky, so he did an odd thing. He put a plastic bag over his head and made a hole in it for his mouth, also produced plastic gloves, and ate the buns this way.

A passenger in the economy class rang the call button in the lavatory. We thought it was some kind of emergency. He politely asked if he could have his meal in there!

A woman had a cat on board that she was breast-feeding! Or trying to.

A very ugly scene ensued at boarding time in Los Angeles, where a passenger had to be "offloaded." He was not happy with his seat, so he yelled at one of the crew members, "Pan Am is the worst airline there is, and you will pay with your *twat!*" He was promptly escorted off the plane.

A clipper-class passenger wanted to use the first-class lavatory. He walked in there without hesitation, and a flight attendant said, "This is first class. Would you mind using the bathroom in clipper class?"

And his answer was, ad verbatim, "So, but I have a first-class prick!"

13

Celebrities

Jocelyne Lagarde was her name, and she was from Tahiti. She was seated in first class of the 707 and weighed about three hundred pounds but looked magnificent and spoke French or English with an accent. She had been one of the Tahitian stars in Marlon Brando's film *Mutiny on the Bounty.* She was my first celebrity on board Pan Am.

She was delightful, chattering away, talking about her weight. She had slimmed down from four hundred pounds. Asked if she intended to lose more, she exclaimed, "Why? I am good now?!"

Famous people behave like everybody else, of course, on an airplane. They sleep, eat, read, talk, go to the bathroom, and get bored—all except Zsa Zsa. She turned the first-class section upside down! And what energy!

This flight became show business; we all played roles in a comical farce. She was very funny and feisty, talking nonstop about her likes and dislikes: "I don't eat croissants!" "What an airline!"; showing me her latest buy, a big, beautiful ring with a diamond; "I bought it myself!" She took all her clothes out of the first-class closet, with a male flight attendant holding up the sleeves at one end and she at the other end to demonstrate the fabric and the style. We were laughing and actually having a pretty good time, although it was a full first-class load with all the other passengers now an audience and with her little mutts running wild all over the first-class cabin in gross violation of the FAA rules. She was accompanied by a few family members and friends, but they just sat there quietly. She was talking happily about sex, how this one and that one was still doing very well in bed.

I had Gina Lollobrigida on board, very dignified and very elegant and very friendly. Just one glass of wine, please. She seemed to be health-conscious and looked very good.

Burt Lancaster was a gentleman, however so much older than we remember him.

Orson Welles required a wheelchair, which it took Pan Am too long (as always!) to produce upon arrival at JFK. Meanwhile, all the ground mechanics came over to shake his hand.

Robert de Niro was one wonderful passenger. I never saw anyone sleep so peacefully throughout an entire flight. We placed one of those quick first-class late snacks (in lieu of dinner service) by his feet, in case he would wake up in the middle of the night. This was a London flight. But he never touched it and had nothing else either. He was doing a Broadway show at the time and was dressed as a rabbi, complete with the sidelocks and all. Upon arrival at Heathrow he just quietly walked off while giving me a cryptical hint of a smile, as if he were saying, "See, nobody recognizes me!" And was that true! Not one single person did, except the other first-class passenger, who had been sitting beside him.

Robert Duvall also was a gem of a passenger, just very pleasant.

Another one I had the enjoyment to spend at least half an hour talking with, was Harvey Keitel. He had finished a while ago filming the movie *The Last Temptation of*

Christ, directed by Martin Scorcese. He said just, "We went there . . . and we did it. . . . " He seemed to enjoy standing there by the 747 aux galley behind first class. He was sexy, very well built, and with an enigmatic aura about him, definitely tricky to figure out. He acted as if he enjoyed "psyching" you a little. I have for many years been a member of the Screen Actors' Guild and worked in at least four hundred films and commercials and industrials both in the capacity of extra player and bit part player and a few speaking parts (with Swedish accents). He asked me what the SAG rate for extra player was today. I told him the minimum was a hundred dollars, but you could make more with overtime and so-called "upgrades." He then said that he started out as an extra and was paid thirty-five dollars for the day!

Other actors and singers I had on board included Harry Belafonte. I still see him coming down the upper-deck staircase in first class with a foul-smelling hot towel. It was moldy, one of Pan Am's shortcomings, when the going got rough.

And Stevie Wonder with his entourage. He spent the entire flight with music headphones to his ears and moving his head rhythmically. He was so patient in view of his blindness. Everybody around him doted on him with obvious love. "We all look alike!" one of them joked, and indeed, a few of them actually did look like "brothers."

My favourite was Maureen O'Hara, once married to the famous Pan Am captain and American folk hero Charlie Blair. The first time I flew with them together was somewhere in the Pacific during the sixties. We were all like a big family and just had a great time on board the airplane. Maureen O'Hara was totally loyal to Pan Am after Charlie Blair's death. She would come on board in first class on the 747, always beautiful, and loved to talk about her late husband and how and what we could do to save Pan Am. She loved to drink white wine and did so with flair and managed to look radiant even at the end of a transatlantic crossing. Once, when she boarded, later, on the much smaller Airbus and I did not recognize her right away, she exclaimed sweetly and disarmingly, "Aren't you going to say hello?!"

I had a number of powerful people on my flights over the years. Barry Goldwater and his wife were seated in the little forward settee lounge on the old 707. That was usually where the crew sat, by the way, when we had our meals and congregated for a while. Passengers sometimes sat there also, if they wanted to talk to us or just be left alone with a book or write on the little table. Mr. Goldwater had been so criticized for his extreme views in the sixties, but he was quite calm and subdued when he sat there, quietly reading a book, and his wife could not have been more gracious.

It was quite an experience to have Henry Kissinger on board an entire Tokyo flight, sometime in the eighties. He was as courteous as could be and excused himself for having laryngitis, his voice even lower and raspier than usual. He drank enormous amounts of tea for his condition. Nancy Kissinger kept to herself, while Kissinger was up and about the cabin having several conversations with other fellow passengers about, you guessed it, political subjects. He spoke openly about America's foreign policies and about the Arabs, too.

Former President Nixon was with us another time. He boarded with a smile on his face, much friendlier than you would expect, and walked with a slight stoop and looked a little shorter and more muscular than his pictures.

And then there was Alan Greenspan, the chairman of

the Federal Reserve. He was gentle and gracious and also looked like he had the world's burdens on his shoulders, which of course he did, at that time especially, sometime in the late eighties. That hangdog look! I think he is admirable and formidable!

There were many more celebrities that I cannot remember anymore. We used to have Elizabeth Taylor all the time, and she was very much liked, down-to-earth, and would visit the cockpit when that was allowed.

One stands out over all the rest though: Mother Theresa. This diminutive lady sat there in first class, "upgraded" of course, a lovely smile on her face, and looked up to you. When offered caviar she first said no, a little embarassed, and then, prompted by her accompanying friend, accepted some on her plate. She was something, her whole face lit with wisdom, kindness, and peace.

14

Pan Am Flight Attendants

There used to be some very good flight attendants. As the years went by, many, many changes took place to the profession, to the "image," and to the flight attendants themselves. The way they looked upon the job and upon themselves was a matter of significance. Generally, it is fair to say, that when we were hired in the sixties and seventies it was a different job than it is today. Unfortunately, we suffered a lot of setbacks along the way, but more about that later.

The way it was. There was no question that some flight attendants were more "professional" than others. Who was the judge of that? Definitely not the public, because the passengers always thought or wrote in their letters to the company that when they had had a "wonderful flight" it was due to the smiles and friendliness and helpfulness of the flight attendants, i.e., "they were so professional!" Although of course it was important to be all of the above, that was far from enough. If management were the judge, I think, they would generally agree with the passengers, in addition to expecting us to perform little miracles on board with our understaffing. In Pan Am they would tell us, "You are only understaffed from your point of view! Things would go smoother if you followed company 'procedures.'" They understood very little about the conditions on the plane, how they changed according to flight, how flexible and almost shrewd you had to be in order to balance off the inadequacies you were often faced with.

If the flight attendants were the judges of what would be "professional," I for one often felt that they were not very good at it either.

Flight attendants at Pan Am were an opinionated lot. They had just as many ideas of how things should be done, what they were supposed to represent, how to do the job, and how to behave on board or elsewhere, for that matter, as the public had or the management or even the press, who wrote about Pan Am all the time. As much as I enjoyed my coworkers during all those years with Pan Am, I remember many an argument by strong-minded individuals, endless discussions about fairly trivial aspects of how the service was supposed to be done, and of course all the union matters.

A "professional" flight attendant was hard to define. It meant many things, skills, for example proficiency in several languages (a requirement to be hired for some). At Pan Am two or more years of college was also a requirement. It meant being safety-conscious all the time, not just on take-off, and being able to handle emergencies on board, whether they were medical or airplane-related, fires on board, etc. It meant knowing exactly how to deliver a "continental" first-class service the Pan Am way, which required a lot more experience than what was offered by the competition at the time. It especially meant solving problems on board. It meant being superflexible and quick to make decisions and even use shrewdness in dealing with passenger problems. There was a lot of smiling and apologizing in the airline business. There was no need to overdo it. In order to be a good flight attendant, friendliness was not enough. You had to be savvy.

Pan Am flight attendants displayed various styles. There was the tempered one, who had an objective view of the job. She did not get emotionally involved and developed a second personality on board to protect against stress. She took a professional distance and therefore had an easier time solving passenger problems. Most flight attendants really did belong in this group. They had outside activities, a full life besides flying. They valued the flying, though knowing full well that the free time they had as well as the privileges they enjoyed would have been impossible in another job.

But then there was the disillusioned one, who possibly suffered from a bit of a lack of self-esteem. She was the exact opposite of the one above. For some reason this type of flight attendant emerged in the midseventies, around the time when the women's movement was becoming an influencing force. She usually felt that the job was not good enough. She should be pursuing a "career" instead. She believed that the media, the public, and management had a low opinion of her, but she could not change her situation, because she did not have the strength to. She would find fault with her coworkers and complain about trivial issues as regarded flying as a whole. The problem was her life, not the job. She was often frumpy-looking, had unkempt hair and no makeup at all, and wore a dirty uniform. She took little pride in her appearance, as if protesting the whole flight attendant "image." She walked around with a perpetual frown on her face and was usually even a lousy worker. She lasted about ten years. In the early eighties new-hires arrived on the scene. There was the social flight attendant who enjoyed the fun part of flying and had a remarkably positive outlook. He or she had everlasting patience with passengers (and crew) and seemed to be floating above it all! He or she enjoyed to the fullest the layovers and did not seem to tire easily. They enjoyed shopping in Rome and Hong Kong and Rio and had friends everywhere they were meeting and greeting. They were doing a million things, like skiing in the Alps, safari in Africa, tripping on the Amazon in South America, sailing and scuba-diving in the Caribbean. They were always suntanned and energetic.

Then there were the entertainers. Humour was the name of the game. Wonderful to work with, to them flying was a job to make fun of, and have fun with. They were for the most part good in the cabin and swept us all along with their spirits. Some of the older male pursers were like that. There was the "Professor," who spoke Russian and Polish and other languages also and delivered nonstop jokes. In his briefings when he would outline the service flow of the meal carts, it went something like this: "We start at the toilets and end up at the kitchen . . . ," gesticulating with his hands. He may have been the one who started the joke about the reply to the passenger who asked him, because he was scratching himself a little, "Pardon me, but do you have hemorrhoids?" which was "If it's not on the menu, we don't have them!" "Sempre Duro" was his trademark idiom, which meant he was always turned on by whatever or whomever, loving life.

There was a type of flight attendant for whom I, personally, had little tolerance: the zealous one. They seemed to be driven by some mysterious force, fuelled by feelings of guilt or masochism or a desire to "correct" procedures and fault other flight attendants. They would drive you crazy with their incessant nervous working drive and would find little "nothings" to occupy themselves with throughout the flight. They would glare at you when you

98

sat down on the jumpseat to have your well-deserved meal. They would insist upon serving soft drinks to passengers again and again after they had already been served. They would fret over little things like if the rolls were soft enough or the portions too small or too big or the napkins folded the right way. They managed to delay the service that way, and many a passenger would fall asleep in first class and clipper class after waiting so long. They were a burden for the purser, whom they would barrage with maintenance items for the logbook to be written up. They never did it themselves or wrote any reports, for that matter, but did not hesitate to voice their complaints loudly. They would goad passengers into writing nice letters about them, giving the impression that they were ever so concerned and caring. Yes, they could be insufferable.

And then there were the lazy ones. Slow and lingering, they would drag themselves through the service, carrying trays or on a cart, and that was it! They did the absolute minimum. There was no initiative, no organisation, no method, no thinking. Since we were so understaffed in Pan Am, this type of flight attendant created a tremendous burden on the rest of the crew. This was half of a worker. However, they did a good job of talking—in the galley, much fussing and discussing about the company, complaining about the union, and so on.

In those days we also had our share of tacky tarts. The skirt was too tight, the hair was bleached too blond and teased high in the sky, the makeup blue or pink or green "shadows" on her face, maybe a run in the stocking. She walked with a slouch and chewed gum! Heaven forbid! Nothing was worse in Pan Am. She was promptly ordered to get rid of the gum or else! When she opened her mouth the words came out, "Ooh, isn't he cute!" or "I just love it here!" or in briefing I remember once this new-hire burst out, "Is Nice in France? Is that where we're going?!" It was like setting off a stink-bomb among the usually sedate crew.

The subservient flight attendant was a problem. She would take a heavy suitbag from a strong male passenger and drag it to the coat closet. She would run for the passenger. She would apologize a lot. Unfortunately, she was also usually female. In those days we were told to apologize for every little thing not perfect, which actually ran contradictory to the proud image of Pan Am. It was a little strange also, since a decade earlier we had the reputation for being snobbish and acting as if we did the passengers a favour by "allowing them on board" and taking part of the magnificent Pan Am experience!

Which takes us to the sophisticated one. This flight attendant does not apologize. In the States this type was not too popular, not too friendly, rather snobbish, they thought. Whereas in Europe, on the Continental airlines like Air France, Alitalia, Lufthansa, and SAS, it was the norm for flight attendants—years ago anyway—to behave most haughtily or at least cooler than their American counterparts. It was unacceptable on the American carriers in the cabins. Nevertheless, in Pan Am we still acted a bit "superior," or call it sophisticated, which was simply a result of flying the world for many years. We were multinational and far more experienced than the rest. The sophistication was an asset. These flight attendants were very good in the cabin. They worked hard and delivered excellent service and had a flair for conversation. They had personality and style and wit, and they always looked good. They were proud to be Pan Am flight attendants.

15

Pan Am Pilots

It was a case of the good, the bad and the ugly. Most Pan Am pilots appeared to be capable in the cockpit and pleasant enough to socialize with. However, we, the flight attendants, often felt that they lived in another world. The cockpit door was like a border between two countries. They dwelled in there quite isolated from people during those long oceanic flights. We, on the other hand, were in constant motion and intermingling with hundreds of people. They worked with instruments, we worked with humans, and pilots and flight attendants never did communicate very well. There were plenty of misunderstandings. In jet recurrent training we were later instructed in how to interact better in emergency situations, should they arise, but I recall many instances where no word from the cockpit was delivered when it was needed, whether it be information about delays on the runway, for example, or, worse, an engine aflame in flight.

On the whole, many of the captains and copilots were completely likeable men, who cared about the crew. They possessed the gift of flexibility. They were not set in their ways. These were the good guys, whom you went to dinner with and partied with. They organised the famous, or infamous, "crew parties" with food and liquor and welcomed everybody and were generous and really fun to be with. They loved to entertain, and they were good communicators, good conversationalists, etc. I remember many layovers that turned into real feasts. However, these pilots became a disappearing breed. It was in the sixties we had all the fun. We flew the 707s in the Pacific with the smaller crews, we all knew each other, and of course we dated one another—a lot. There was a lot of drinking—it went with the tropical climates we flew to.

Many crew members ended up in bed together, whether it was under the influence of just wine or "Rusty Nails" or simply the seductive atmosphere of the lush and very beautiful islands we spent our layovers on. It was romantic, that was the difference. It was so romantic. Nobody worried about diseases or gossip or other evil consequences. You were supposed to have fun, play as much as possible. It was benevolent and quite innocent. We also got away with a lot. Today there would be mass firings for the rules we broke. I remember one flight attendant who had to have oxygen in the cockpit the next day after a wild night. She had been fed "milk shakes" consisting of vodka, brandy, some kind of tropical juice, and half and half by the captain himself. He was also the one who supplied the oxygen. Never mind; he was smiling, she was still smiling, and everybody else did, too. This was the sixties, so besides liquor there was also plenty of marijuana, hash, and other substances available. Dexedrine, "uppers," were in easy supply. Some of the crew found them "necessary" to stay awake during those long flights after all that "crew-partying"! Shocking, maybe, but that was the way it was.

The seventies changed all that. The pilots and the flight attendants were not flying together so much anymore. The 747s had arrived and with them the new-hires in those days could care less about pilots. They were "too old"! After only four years of flying, I myself felt terribly "senior." At that time I became a purser, and along with me was a friend who exclaimed in the training class for the "upgraded" pursers, "Here we are, old and wrinkled!" We were twenty-seven years old. With the 747 flying and being transferred to New York, I now had my encounters with a different type of pilot.

On my first flight out of New York, two things gave me a shock. First, I could not believe passengers were ordering Bloody Marys in the morning! On my Pacific flights the drinking was done in the evening, for heaven's sake. That had been "civilised." What was this? And call buttons! Nobody had rung a call button before on my flights. My second shock was when this call button was rung, not by a passenger, but, lo and behold, by a pilot, a coworker, an employee of the airline. I thought it was an emergency, but all he wanted was coffee! Why did he not come out and get it himself, like they had always done before? No, they were too "busy," and besides, they were accustomed to service! No, this was Pan Am, and the captains reigned supreme. "El Supremo," they were nicknamed, or it was drummed into us; "The captain is God!" In the Pacific that had been true also, but never taken so seriously. New York was humourless, the pilots were unsmiling, and with the 747 it was joked, "There were captains who walked up the stairs to the upper deck and the cockpit and never came down."

They did not come down; they were the prima donnas. Here are my stories:

The prima donnas demanded to be served first class exactly like the passengers, not just the food, but course by course. In view of our understaffing, it was preposterous. Many an argument ensued about this during flights and on the ground. Pan Am pilots got used to this service mainly because the Pan Am captains had been such tyrants in the old flying boat days, so this was a leftover situation from the old days, but also because the female (*not* the male) flight attendants, unfortunately, catered to them. It became a habit, which was unfortunate. As a purser I would sometimes need more help in the cabin, and here was the first-class galley attendant in the cockpit running back and forth with dishes. It did infuriate me. Here I was faced with demanding first-class passengers, understaffing, a reluctant flight attendant, as well as cantankerous pilots, who neither said "thank you" for all that extra service nor understood an iota about what was going on in the cabin. Their ears were deaf to my complaints. Some of them were also so badly behaved that they did not hesitate to pick at the dishes set up nicely on the serving carts in first class. We used to smack them lightly over their hands like you do to children and utter, "That's a no-no!" A heated argument between me and a 747 captain went on before take-off in Tokyo. I remember he had white hair and he pointed his finger at me, saying, "If I don't get served at the same time as the passengers, you are offloaded, understood!" "Offloaded" meant he actually had the authority to remove me from the flight, if his wishes were not met. I had explained to him that it was impossible to serve the cockpit at the same time as the passengers, since there were only two flight attendants on the upper deck of the 747 with up to twenty first-class passengers, and in Pan Am, as I have said, this service was a seven-cart course-by-course presentation that took up to three to four hours, which should have required four flight attendants to do gracefully. He had no consideration for that. Downstairs there were thirty-six first-class passengers, two separate sections, with only three flight attendants!

I wanted to spit at him. Instead I glared. He glared

back. I did not want to remain in Tokyo. As usual, "God" won. I wrote a report to the company, and as usual, nothing was changed. If we were understaffed, that was from "your point of view."

Another situation I will not forget involved another inflated ego, who demanded service, not for himself, though. The flight engineer on this 747 came down to the lower galley to get some coffee. This was also on the ground before boarding. The galley attendant showed him where to get it. This one was at a loss how to do it (!). When he asked again, she showed him again, while she was busy organising the galley. He got his coffee, went up the stairs. A few minutes later the captain came storming down, during boarding now, red in the face, and demanded loudly that I, the purser, switch positions with the other purser in the main cabin. (There were always two pursers, one in the front, one in the back.) I should have overseen that the galley attendant serve the engineer personally! He had obviously been looking forward to dinner in the sky and did not want to be served by a purser or a galley attendant, who already were showing signs of unwillingness! We, the pursers, switched positions back and forth several times, and I still ended up in my original position in first class. It was ridiculous; what a dance. I had to write yet another report about a trivial matter, this time to the chief pilot and my union and the pilots' union. At Pan Am we were always writing reports.

One prima donna demanded lobster. The first-class orders were already taken, no lobster left. He screamed at the alarmed flight attendant, "I am the most important person on this plane, and I get what I want!" I don't remember if we had to "unorder" the passenger's selection.

It sounds incredible, but there actually was one crazy captain who insisted that the serving carts be rolled into the cockpit (!) like in the cabin. I can imagine what the FAA would say about that! They do not even allow glassware in there.

Another tale: A flight attendant went into the cockpit to take the meal orders, this time after the passengers. She was told by the captain, "I'll take the roast beef, and I'll take it now!"

She had none left. "Can I give you something else?" she politely asked.

Unbelievably, he shouted, "Goddammit, you f——ing bitch, get out there and get me the roast beef!"

Just before landing he shouted again, "I am God on this airplane, and you do what I tell you!"

They were just approaching descent, but the captain was not in his seat but in the galley making waves. So she said, "Listen, God, the plane might crash if you don't go up there and do your job, because we are just about to land." It was said that he apologised when she threatened to report him.

There were some pilots we called the Flying Cowboys. They were the ones who used to call you "gals," and they did have swaggering walks. They were not typical of Pan Am, though. They manoeuvred the plane rather roughly, yanking at the controls, the plane jerking from side to side on the taxiway, screeching halts, even rough flights. They landed with a bang. Some landings were so hard in the sixties, as well as into the eighties, that oxygen masks fell down over passengers' heads and overhead bins with all the paraphernalia in there came crashing down, galley carts were broken away from the supports, and the latches gave, sending them right out into the aisles, leaking toilets and galleys overflowing, sending torrents of liquid into the carpeted aisles, soiling them even more. There were plenty of lawsuits. On one of my hard-landing flights a woman's head was injured by a flyaway cart, resulting in legal action, not by her, oddly enough, but by the passenger across from her.

There were the tightwads. I never understood why pilots were so stingy. They made over $100,000 a year in those days, but at the dinner table in the restaurants all over the world they would complain about how expensive it was. The check was divided precisely, but sometimes only in their favour. Here were the flight attendants making $25,000 a year and eating sometimes half of what the pilots had. "Let's split it equally," they suggested. Not very gentlemanly. When the flight attendants protested, they were told not to be petty. They were the junior ones, who did not know. The pilots often got a tongue-lashing by the seniors. As the years went by, the more senior we became, the more we told them off.

Pilots, like the rest of us, had to give their share of concessions when Pan Am started to slide. They did not like it one bit. "I would have to curtail my antique car collection!" one of them had the gall to say. Some junior flight attendants qualified for food stamps in the eighties after an up to twenty-five percent salary reduction. This was embarrassing to the company, so a few dollars were "adjusted." The tightwads, in spite of their generous pay, were quick to point out that it was in perfect order that they should be getting a raise while the rest of us could do just fine on $20,000 a year. "It takes the smarts!" one of them pointed out to me.

They were also stingy with the cabin air in flight. We had ozone problems in those days. It was hard to breathe on the polar flights, both on the 707s and on the 747SPs (special performance aircraft used for long-range flights to Tokyo, e.g.). A severely restricting feeling welled in your throat and chest due to ozone. This situation eventually was cleared away, and we could breathe again. However, on many flights the oxygen flow was inadequate. Some planes were worse than others. There were adjustments the pilots could do, but often they refused, either because they were told to conserve fuel or because they simply did not believe that crew members in the cabin were uncomfortable. They pooh-poohed us. Some airplanes had "airpacks," and if they were turned on, we got more air circulation. One purser went into the cockpit to ask that they be turned on. Both passengers and crew were feeling ill. This jackass captain told the purser, "If you do this, exercise like this [and he demonstrated with his arms and hands], it does two things: it develops your breath and develops your bust!"

Well, that was history. The prima donnas, the cowboys, the tightwads and the jackasses disappeared mostly with the decline of Pan Am. At the end of the eighties it seemed to come full-circle. The good guys were in a majority again. Rarely a hard landing; on the contrary, the landings were magnificently smooth for the most part. There even seemed to be less turbulence in flight! No scrambled eggs on the ceiling anymore. I don't know what they were suddenly doing right. They became more curteous. I don't recall one single temper tantrum in the cockpit during the late eighties. Pan Am was bleeding; the pilots were more careful and more disciplined for sure. Everybody was worried about their jobs. There was more camraderie amongst the crews. A "we are in this together" kind of attitude developed, and that even included management to a certain degree.

16

Management

I never met Juan Trippe, the founder of Pan Am. I would have liked to. He ruled Pan Am when I was hired in 1966. He was the one who created Pan Am, its greatness, its glamour, and its worldwide reputation. When I was growing up all over the world, it was Pan Am, the elitist airline, I wanted to work for. So I am glad there was a Juan Trippe, who created that for me.

He was succeeded by Najeeb Halaby in the early seventies, a nice man, who had Washington connections. But Washington did not like Pan Am, it was said, so we were always ignored by whatever president was in the White House and by the senators and the congressmen, who favoured the "domestic" airlines like American and United.

Pan Am wanted domestic "feeder flights" to their international routes, but none was forthcoming. There was so much talk about it. "If only we had domestic flights!" It could solve Pan Am's financial problems. Then later on: "If only the fuel was not so expensive!"

And again: "The competition is killing us. How dare they [the "other" American airlines] encroach upon our territory!" Deregulation had settled in. It turned out to be the nemesis of the entire airline industry. And finally: "It's the unions! The labour unions, you flight attendants and pilots and mechanics! You are the source of our problems. You cost too much!" We were still costing too much after 20–25 percent paycuts and frozen pensions (in 1984) and numerous concessions over the years. We were being blamed over and over again for Pan Am's financial woes.

Pan Am became the airline of excuses.

We were pretty sick and tired of hearing about how it was our fault when management did not mind giving themselves raises in the financially strapped Pan Am and asking us for yet another giveback.

Halaby was replaced by former air force general William T. Seawell, who was Pan Am's chairman in the seventies and into the eighties. He was rumoured to be both cold and temperamental. He fired people in management and cleaned house, at least for a while. Pan Am had always had a case of "vice presidentitis," it was joked. Too many vice presidents, who had been largely inefficient and certainly were overpaid for what they produced. These management princes had parties all around town. There were friends of mine at the time who ran into these guys at cocktail parties where they boasted about how they were Pan Am vice presidents but did nothing at all. One of them remarked to a friend of mine how "the Pan Am stewardesses are so spoiled, they have it so good! Those girls!"

Pan Am was used as an example at the Harvard School of Business Administration of how a company should not be run. It was "top heavy" with too many vice presidents.

Seawell was succeeded by C. Edward Acker from Texas in the mideighties. He was different altogether, not a graduate from any of the eastern colleges, no refined manners or haughty demeanor—not a snob. He was "streetwise." He also cleaned house. "Who is in charge here?" he would call out disdainfully. In the financially ailing Pan Am he gave us all hope in the beginning. We became "Acker Backers" and wore pins on the lapels to that effect.

Acker and his wife liked "D.P. on the rocks." Flight service had never heard of anything like it, although we were slowly becoming all too familiar with the "folksy" terminology. Translated into world language, it was the champagne Dom Perignon, but on ice! Please! This was too much. But he was the chairman of Pan Am, so he got his D.P. on the rocks. What we had less tolerance for, however, was when our chairman and his wife allegedly disembarked with a few of the above-mentioned bottles in hand. We would have been fired for stealing champagne, and some were.

He certainly was outspoken and brash, our Acker. He was fun for awhile. Then he sold the Pacific routes. Just like that! To United Airlines. How could he! They were profitable! They were Pan Am's territory! They made money!

However, people forgot and just refused to remember how close we were to going under. In the Flight Service Department they hated him for doing that, because now the Pacific flying was over, an era of flying had come to an end.

I think I am one of the few employees who actually still today give Acker credit for what he did. Sure, they were moneymaking routes, but we were down and out. We had sold everything: the Continental hotels, the Pan Am Building in New York, and other route systems, and yet there was simply no money. The Pacific routes gave Pan Am an immediate cash infusion and made it possible to survive yet another few years. It was just so amazing, Pan Am would sell some assets, continue flying for another five years or so, then sell some more assets, and continue on and on like that for many years. The financially strapped Pan Am! Anything that would keep our jobs for a while longer was welcome. If Acker had not sold those routes at that particular time, we would have managed to lose money on those routes anyway. Unfortunately Pan Am was very good at losing money. Why? One of the reasons I believe was because they simply wasted so much. It was the waste and the lack of organisation, the lack of controlling the costs. As I mentioned earlier, Pan Am would have to pay fifteen dollars for an extra lemon to be picked up by the Mob-controlled JFK trucks. That is the way it was all over the system. Pan Am was being overcharged for services and equipment, and they could not control their costs. There was a lack of follow-through. For example, they decided to install netting material over the overhead bins on the 747s to prevent items from falling out when the bins were opened. (There had been so many lawsuits.) Only some airplanes were outfitted. It was too costly, so it was stopped, never completed. It also turned out that it was the wrong overhead bins that were being netted. It was the middle bins, that were slanted, where things fell out and hurt people, not the side bins, where the netting was being installed. There were many half-baked procedures like that, expensive and wasteful.

So when Acker sold the Pacific routes, why did he not pay off some of Pan Am's debt, stop the waste, control costs? Instead, what happened? The money from those routes just seemed to fritter away somewhere, nowhere. Even when Pan Am was profitable, where did the money go? The debts never seemed to be paid off. Pan Am's pension liabilities were in the many millions, and then Acker did a painful thing. He froze the pensions in 1984! I could never understand how it could be legal to freeze pensions for the employees. Now we ended up with a fraction of the original sum we were supposed to have gotten in our retirement. How would you like to end up with only $150 a month after working for twenty-five years for a company that you gave your lifeblood to? All of those chairmen and vice presidents, on the other hand, departed Pan Am rich with millions after "visiting" only for a few years at the helm.

The last chairman was Tom Plaskett who came from American Air Lines, in my opinion the most civilised man of them all. He gave the impression of gentleness and fairness. Some said that he was ineffectual or had too little "drive." However, if he had succeeded in merging Pan Am with Northwest at the time, which he tried so desperately to do and was so close to that amazing deal—linking two major airlines with perfectly coordinated routes, the Atlantic with the Pacific (again), domestic and international routes, complementing each other—I think he was the one who would have been hailed as something of a hero.

Unfortunately for Pan Am, he failed, but he was so close. If he had succeeded in that venture, I believe Pan Am would be flying today. It was exactly what Pan Am needed, that type of merger. I think his efforts were downplayed in the ensuing years.

Instead Delta Air Lines made its entrance a little later, but that is another story.

17

Emergency on Board

In all the twenty-five and a half years I flew for Pan Am, I never had a real emergency. That tells one something about airline safety. However, I had plenty of so-called "potential" emergencies. Potential emergencies can be cabin fires or engine fires in flight, a landing gear that does not lower, a suspected bomb on board, etc. It's a situation where you may have to prepare for an emergency evacuation or just be on the alert.

The "primary function of the flight attendant," according to the FAA, is to "ensure the safety of the passengers" in an emergency. The FAA states further that one flight attendant should be responsible for fifty passengers and that three-quarters of the emergency exits on any given airplane have to be covered by an FAA-qualified flight attendant, who also has to be qualified on that particular aircraft.

In Pan Am we were trained very well. We were vigilant throughout the flight with seat belts and the smoking rules and cabin luggage to the point of zealousness. Also, because Pan Am was so often tragically the target of terrorist attacks, we learned both in training and on the line how to spot suspicious passenger behaviour. A flight would often be delayed because of unclaimed passenger bags in the cabin or a passenger missing, who should have been on board according to the departure report. If he was missing, the entire cargo load of suitcases would have to be searched in order to remove this passenger's bag. There were no computers at the time, and frankly, ground security left a lot to be desired, as far as I could tell. Pan Am's security force, the so-called "Alert" system, appeared to be somewhat lax, the people trained very hastily, paid minimum wages for an extremely responsible job, a matter of life and death. History has now shown through the discoveries and the lawsuits resulting from the Lockerbie tragedy that that was indeed the case.

So it did not matter how vigilant we were on board the airplane. On the ground there were too many signs of negligence. Every time we boarded an international flight, this fear and lack of trust in proper security was at least in the back of my mind.

At JFK also for a few years there was a succession of bomb scares, and boardings were interrupted or the passengers were asked to disembark after they had boarded. Many grumbled and protested loudly. I could not understand at the time why people reacted so negatively when it would be their own safety that was compromised. It took years for the public to learn how real the terrorist threats had become, and today finally, in the USA, people are far more security-conscious.

At Pan Am the safety training we received, when we were hired, was only the beginning. Like all other American carriers we were required to attend yearly refreshers, so-called Jet Emergency Recurrent Training. At Pan Am it started out as once a year and then later became twice a year because of the increasing terrorism all over the world. At these refresher courses you had to pass written exams of fifty or sixty questions and watch horrifying videos of airplane crashes, fires, decompressions, and even how bombs were made. It really was quite depressing to see all that blackened airplane wreckage and bloody bodies. We studied first aid and also became certified in CPR. We had drills a hundred times in evacuating different types of aircraft and learned how important the evacuation commands to passengers were in these situations. It's not just a matter of getting out. It is how to get out, how to avoid smoke and fire, which exits to use, how to slide down the chutes, whether to turn left or right on the wings, how to get into a life raft, what types of life rafts, how to inflate the life jackets and when, how to behave in a smoke-filled cabin, what to do in a decompression. Most people do not know that in a decompression, the airplane goes into a steep descent from a high altitude to one much lower (14,000 feet). At that time, unsecured items could be crashing all over the place, and if standing, you could lose your foothold, and those galley carts, God forbid, could be racing into the aisles. I never had a decompression, but I heard about them.

Nobody liked to attend those training classes. We used to say it was "the worst day or days of the entire year," but it was absolutely necessary. Although we were very safety-conscious in Pan Am, some crews still forgot why they were on the airplane. They sometimes became obsessed with the service procedures and were not alert enough on take-offs and landings. Even if no food or drink was ever served on board, you still had to have the required number of FAA-qualified flight attendants on every single flight just to be present, emergency or not.

The exams we had to pass were not too difficult. However, they could be very tricky, with multiple-choice questions, and it was often a matter of the correct words being used, technical words like *bustle* or *bulkhead, arming lever* or *deployment handle, beacon radios* or *VHF transmitters, red indicators* or *green arrows*. It was a matter of pushing the pin or pulling the pin to the left or to the right, upwards or downwards, aft or forward, outboard or inboard! The location questions were difficult. It was not enough to know where all the different extinguishers, oxygen bottles, life rafts, megaphones, first-aid kits and smoke goggles were. You had to memorise the precise location. Was the spare life vest in a pouch under your seat forward or aft of some other equipment, above the floor or next to the floor? In case of a darkened or smoke-filled cabin, by feeling your way via the equipment you could save lives.

In Pan Am we had before every single flight a rather thorough emergency briefing also. We would even ask questions of one another. Incidentally, if you did not pass your emergency test, you could be removed temporarily from the payroll and taken off flight status until you were requalified. It was all very embarrassing if you failed the tests and cause for much anxiety.

My potential emergency situations in flight were the following: The worst time I ever had on Pan a Am flight was not even an incident but a horrifying experience, which was a "freak" storm that hit us upon landing in Philadelphia. It was a charter flight from Shannon, Ireland, sometime in the midseventies. Although not even a thunderstorm, this monster pelted us around for about two hours! I don't know what they were up to in either the cockpit or the ATC (the air traffic control), but we were trying to land. However, all other aircraft had diverted, except one single plane, an Allegheny aircraft. That pilot could not even hold the microphone steady in front of his face, and the instrument indicators were going haywire, gyrating wildly back and forth. Six times we tried to land, two hours of hell in the cabin with pieces of luggage and

117

galley items hitting the ceiling numerous times. Even the heavy wine cooler went halfway up in the air. We had had little time to secure things. I was on the back jumpseat of the 707 holding hands with the other flight attendant. It was hard to keep from screaming; the lower part of my spine was pierced with pain from the tension. The adult men were screaming, though. Many of them had been drinking quite a lot during the flight, and here they sobered quickly. We would climb to one altitude, then circle around there for a while, and then we would descend into hell again, six times, and be tossed around like a leaf in a blustery autumn wind. "Captain, what are you doing?" my coworker kept repeating over and over again. The nightmare finally ended. We diverted to Washington. Passengers and crew were still shaking upon disembarking. Nobody had gotten hurt, but of course many had gotten sick, and the cabin did not smell too good.

Afterwards when I was talking to the pilots, they said that there had been a certain "lack of communication" between them and the ATC. It was the first officer who had been at the controls and who had landed. He had taken over the plane from the captain for some reason. He said, that he had not been through anything like this since the military.

A few months later I received a letter from Pan Am about this flight. Enclosed was another letter from the charter group thanking the crew for landing us safely in Washington.

The Pan Am 747s had engine troubles all the time. It was an often-repeated phrase: "We lost an engine" after take-off or halfway through the flight. "Losing" an engine meant that it had malfunctioned, stopped. The flight usually continued on course with three engines, the faulty engine was restarted, or sometimes the flight was diverted. When this happened in flight, you could feel it. There could be a popping sound and/or strange vibrations. It was not so bad to lose one engine, but if you lost two or three, you did have an emergency. The plane could fly on one engine, but it meant trouble. I experienced six engine failures during the course of only one and a half years. During that time, in the mideighties, Pan Am, as usual strapped for cash, had changed its maintenance procedures from "defensive" to "acute," which meant that only the most severe maintenance problems were taken care of. Also, like Eastern Air Lines, it was rumoured, the maintenance logs were checked off OK, but repairs had not been made. The FAA was checking us of course, but I remember several pilots at the time who were lamenting, "I wish they would check Pan Am like they did Eastern!" Eastern had gotten in trouble for many maintenance infractions. Pan Am did not.

I don't really know why I was so "lucky," flying with engines aflame, one after the other.

It happened late in the evening on take-off from JFK on this flight bound for Rio de Janeiro. I heard a "boom," and there was the right outboard engine on fire. Well, all we did was circle around for an hour and then return to JFK. The fire was extinguished in flight. We boarded another plane.

Another time it happened between London and Frankfurt. It went "pop." There were also flames, but you could not see them due to the daylight. The passengers had no idea what was taking place, and they could not at first understand why we were diverting back to London. As often was the case, the cockpit was a little slow in relaying the information.

Another time it happened was right in the middle of the Atlantic between London and New York. It was quite dramatic, and I was definitely nervous. The left inboard engine was suddenly engulfed in flames. Passengers were sleeping mostly, and there were very few of them, a light load, stretched out over the seats, lying down. That was why they never knew what was taking place outside the windows on the left side. One man, however, sat there in his seat by the window and stared in disbelief at the flames but said absolutely nothing. I mentioned to him that I was going to call the cockpit and that the airplane could fly just fine on three engines.

I waited awhile. I thought the cockpit would make an announcement, but none came. I did not want to disturb them. The other flight attendants were in various stages of alertness or alarm, but some completely indifferent or even unnoticing. The 747 is a very big airplane, and most of the time the people at one end have no idea what is going on at the other end. In the back they were, as usual, engaged in conversation and never did find out what was going on until after the flight had arrived in London!

Since the flames were raging for at least a few minutes and no word from the cockpit, I picked up the interphone. I said, "What about this fire . . . ?"

A wretched and irate voice shot back, "Yeah, we know!"

After another few minutes the fire was out. The pilots had "closed the engine down." Later in the flight they restarted it, and it was OK. I don't think their way of communicating had been OK.

We had plenty of minor incidents on board Pan Am, which I don't see anymore today. Some passengers did not like to fasten their seat belts. There were all kinds of minor injuries due to turbulence. On the runway after landing a man stood up to gather his belongings, the plane came to a sudden halt, which is what happens so often while taxiing, and the man crashed with a bang into the cockpit door on the 707. The door held, but the man was visibly shaken, not hurt. Passengers finally did learn to stay in their seats.

It happened once also that a flight took off again after landing, while passengers were standing in the aisles, thinking they were about to disembark. It happened without warning. Obviously another plane was taking off or landing on the same runway.

There were near-misses all the time. You heard about them.

Here are excerpts of wires for the pilots, which they received at the time about some close calls:

IN THE LAST YEAR ALONE . . . 8 MIDAIR COLLI-SIONS WERE AVERTED ONLY BY VIGILANT PAN AM CREWS, WHO TOOK EVASIVE ACTION IN THE FEW REMAINING SECONDS BEFORE IMPACT. IN MOST CASES ACT HAD ERRED AND IT WAS THE FLIGHT CREWS . . . THE LAST LINE OF DEFENSE . . . WHO PREVENTED DISASTER. SEVERAL YEARS AGO . . . TWO PAN AM WIDEBODY JETS COLLIDED AFTER BEING CLEARED INTO THE SAME AIRSPACE OFF THE FLORIDA COAST. ONLY THE FIRST OFFICER'S VIGILANCE AND QUICK ACTION AVERTED A MIDAIR.

And windshear:

THE FIRST MICROBURST ALERT ISSUED INDI-CATED A 35-KT LOSS . . . INTENSIFYING TO 95 KTS IN APPROXIMATELY 2 MINUTES.

ONE AIRLINE PILOT . . . UPON RECEIVING A 60-KT LOSS MICROBURST ALERT AT THE 3-MILE FINAL POINT . . . MADE AN IMMEDIATE AVOIDANCE DECI-SION . . . APPLYING GO-AROUND POWER AND

STARTING A CLIMB AT APPROXIMATELY 600 FT AGL
AT 1000 FT AGL . . . HE RECEIVED AN 80-KT LOSS
ALERT . . . EXPERIENCING A 50-KT LOSS IN AIR-
SPEED AND 400-FT LOSS IN ALTITUDE BEFORE EX-
ITING THE SHEAR SAFELY AND SUCCESSFULLY.
FLIGHT SAFETY AND COMMUNICATIONS.

Emergencies on board also included the medical variety, which were far more prevalent. In the course of my
twenty-five and a half years with Pan Am I must have
administered oxygen on board at least a hundred times to
sick passengers. Whether it was just too much alcohol or
a serious medical condition, the airplane cabin air and
constricted seating arrangements always aggravated the
situation. So oxygen was very much needed and improved
the condition almost immediately. It was even used for
anxiety. When the passenger was given oxygen and clothing was loosened, he or she felt better. Flight attendants
were trained in first aid, so that was all we could do. If the
condition was really serious, a doctor or nurse or other
medical professional was paged over the PA system. This
happened quite often. I remember this poor man on a flight
to Puerto Rico who was overcome with terrible stomach
pains. A nurse was summoned, but all she could do was
talk to him. At the time we did not have a special medical
kit on board, just a first-aid kit, so therefore no medication.

That was also the tragic case for the one passenger I
had who died. It was just before landing in Dahran, Saudi
Arabia. It happened at breakfast time in first class. The
passenger next to him alerted me to this man's strange
behaviour. I looked at this older Saudi-Arabian man. He
was so still, his eyes flickering a little, and then nothing,
no movement. At least three doctors were there. They said
that without adrenaline he could not be revived. One of

them could not believe that there was no such medical equipment on board. I had suggested CPR, but that would have accomplished nothing according to this doctor.

After a few years, medical kits containing drugs, stethoscope, blood pressure cuff, etc., were installed in the cockpits on all aircraft.

18

Image Blues

From the time I was hired by Pan Am in 1966 and for the next twenty-five years that I flew, I experienced the ups and downs of the social status of the flight attendant. At the time of hiring, we had been so conditioned into taking great care at representing the "Pan Am image," which was supposedly conservative, responsible, and worldly. As the years went by, a fundamental change took place, started mostly by the "other" American airlines. We found ourselves at Pan Am being brought down to earth, dragged down from our lofty skies to the folksy, average-man passenger loads we now had to serve. One of us pointedly remarked that you had to "lower yourself to their standards."

The new passengers would refer to the economy class or the main cabin as "coach," and first class and clipper class were overflowing with "upgrades" from economy. These passengers did not know what caviar was, and explaining cheeses and wines to them, as well as international landing cards, could become very trying. Maybe we were snobbish, but if you spoke several languages and flew around the world like other people go to the office in the morning, you could not help but grow a little impatient at times when the captain made an announcement over the

PA system telling us that we were flying over the Shetland Islands and people would ask, "What's that?"

Flying would never be what it once was, and we could thank the Airline Deregulation Act of 1978 for that. A new era had settled in. Enter the cheap fares, the cheap airlines, the "Greyhound" passengers, and the low-paid flight attendants! It was not just cheap; it was rock bottom!

I can think of few occupations that were struck by such a slide in prestige. Once in a while we were allocated the term *safety professionals,* invented by American Air Lines flight attendants. Still, the public, especially in the USA, thought of us as mere "attendants." "A flight attendant is someone who hands me a pillow," said one hairdresser in New York!

An article appeared about ten years ago in the *Airport Press* under the heading "Airline Workers: Flight's Fallen Angels" (reprinted by permission):

Once they were "sky girls," nurses hired to reassure a nervous public. In the 1950s they were another sort of marketing device—sort of sorority sweethearts, the vestal virgins of the air. They lost the virgin part in the "I'm Cheryl: Fly Me" era of the sixties and seventies, yet always they seemed glamorous. But deregulation changed that too. As they have slashed costs, the airlines have also been dismantling the dashing imagery they so carefully floated over the years.

In Pan Am we may not have been "vestal virgins" or "Fly Me" types, but it was still an American airline influenced by the rest. Wherever we flew in the rest of the world, though, we were still envied when we walked by in our ice blue gabardine uniforms, white gloves, and hats. We were not "sky girls" but "fly ladies." A magazine article written by Peter Wilkinson titled "Pan Am: The Fall of a Legend," which first appeared in *Condé Nast Traveler,* sums it up (reprinted by permission):

> "We thought we were it, and we were," said a woman who was a Pan Am flight attendant for twenty-nine years. "The company told you you'd made it big, and it was extremely glamorous—a pretty hot-shot job." Stewardesses stayed at Frank Lloyd Wright's Imperial Hotel in Tokyo and danced at the Rainbow Room during New York layovers. They lingered in Fiji and Australia long enough to sightsee and shop, and they visited the Chinese Opera in Hong Kong, opium dens in Bangkok and the gold markets in Beirut.

No wonder, then, that when low-fare airlines like People Express appeared on the scene, the flight attendant image took a nosedive along with the flight attendant pay.

It was too bad! The salaries were slashed, i.e., the B-scale pay was invented (same work for less money for new-hires), the workload heavily increased with passengers who could now afford to fly. In the ensuing dog-eat-dog price competition, it soon meant dog-eat-employees. It was like being hit with a sledgehammer. We were unionised of course, but how much could a union do when the airline was hemorrhaging? You were lucky enough to have a job! The public loved the deregulated skies of course—at our expense. We were more understaffed in Pan Am than ever, but the demands on us increased all the more. We ran in the aisles to get the service done, our uniforms got soiled, our faces looked harried and worn, and we were angry most of the time. It was very unfair.

The *Airport Press* article went on to note: "With recession, high fuel prices and the stark defeat of the air controllers' strike added to the mixture, the early years of deregulation were something of a bloodbath—some 15,000 airline jobs were eliminated in 1980 alone."

"The role of the professional flight attendant is in danger of disappearing," said an official of what was left of Continental's stewardess union. "What they want is $4.50-an-hour waitresses. It's appalling."

Continental was perhaps the extreme example. Frank Lorenzo bought that airline, put it into bankruptcy, broke the labour contracts, fired two-thirds of the employees, and paid those remaining about two-thirds less money. Nice man! How we hated him! One Continental stewardess, when asked what it was like to work for Frank Lorenzo, replied unforgettably, "It's like being forced to dance with the man who raped you."

Well, People Express did not last. Neither did many others of the "upstart" airlines. The article goes on to say: "And once ticket prices start to rise, the airlines may work at putting some of the glamour back into flying, maybe more than we ever wanted. The flight attendant may get a new designer uniform, and she may serve fine wines. But don't expect her to smile. She'll be thinking about next month's rent."

At Pan Am we gave a lot of thought to the next month's rent or mortgage payment. We worried about our jobs for so many years. Paradoxically, we never believed that Pan Am could go under. Nobody did. It was the case of the perennially financially ailing Pan Am. Our union, the IUFA, the Independent Union of Flight Attendants, managed to win some remarkable gains during our contract negotiations, due mainly to the skills of our negotiating committee, consisting of hard-bargaining flight attendants. If it had not been for them, we would easily have found ourselves in the same situation as Continental Air Lines. I remember very well how management proposed

127

slashing our pay to dirt-wage level and increasing the flying time requirement to the point of health hazards and safety compromising status.

Our image was not helped very much by the women's movement, although originally it had forced the airlines to allow us to keep flying if we married or got pregnant and the age limit was abolished. Male flight attendants were hired, which altered the image into more "neutral." At the same time the term *flight attendant* also was invented. It was supposedly less sexist. However, I always felt that the term was a bit of a put-down, sort of like "gas station attendant."

The new German word for the occupation was better, *Flugbegleiter,* which meant "flight escorter." It could not be used in English, but what about *flight agent* or even *flight service agent* I used to think. I gave up thinking about it, because nobody was interested, least of all flight attendants.

The women's movement served as no advocate for flight attendants as it grew stronger. We were being excluded; our job was not a "career." We also still suffered from the trite old stereotyped sexy role syndrome, which was anathema to women's lib. What a drag it was to read in women's magazines about how flight attendants only "catered" to men, as if we had time to differentiate between passengers of different sexes! In another article in the same magazine would be advice on how to behave on the road for businesswomen on trips, when you were "alone" in hotels, and the like. If anyone knew what it was like to be a lone woman "on the go" it was flight attendants, whom lone women travellers could take pointers from. We were the ones who had stayed in hotels for many, many years. We could tell them about how to pack for cold weather and hot weather, what to eat and drink, which inoculations were required for what countries, how to behave with porters and waiters, and all of the other little "excellent tips for travel" that were so eagerly pointed out in the articles.

It was assumed that flight attendants had no interest in career advancement or corporate climbing—which was exactly right—for the most part. However, there were advancement opportunities, if you chose to take that path. You became a supervisor if you were good and showed a lot of interest, and then definitely could advance further, and many did. Nevertheless, most of us felt that we had better lives than someone who was working nine to five every day. We did not envy the career women or men. We enjoyed flying—still. So what was the point of climbing the corporate ladder? We were making the same amount of money as in management; at least the senior flight attendants and the pursers were.

The curious thing about flying was that it must have been the only occupation where people willingly gravitated downwards to a lower position. Pursers frequently "downgraded" to flight attendant, because they were weary of the many aggravations that came with being in the leadership role, and it could be easier to be awarded a wider choice of desirable trips due to the seniority and scheduling system. Supervisors went back "on the line," because they wanted to fly, have more flexible hours, and perhaps flee the corporate rat race.

Working Woman had a salary survey every year of women's jobs, but flight attendants were impolitely excluded as well as secretaries, models, and actresses!

Didn't we count? Didn't we read *Working Woman?*

I decided to write them a letter, either to remind them of our existence or just for fun:

Dear *Working Woman,*

Why have you excluded the position of flight attendant from your survey? Do unionised employees not count, or do you still believe, that flying is not a "real" job?

The pay for a senior flight attendant is $28,000–$43,000 a year (starting salary is about $20,000). That is quite a bit more than some of the jobs listed in your survey.

This was sometime in the eighties. The pay does not sound like so much today, but at that time it was not bad at all, very competitive with that of other jobs. Then shortly thereafter came all the pay cuts of course in the industry. And the lay-offs, and the cutbacks, and the concessions, and on and on.

The glamour was out, the turbulence was in.

19

Why Did Pan Am Have to Fold?

"The World's Most Experienced Airline," the once elite and glamorous and most worldwide carrier of them all, was on its way down. From taking off in the thirties and the forties, cruising beautifully in the fifties and sixties, changing altitude in the seventies and early eighties, Pan Am was now in a landing pattern and finally touched down, grounded for good, on December 4, 1991.

The reasons for Pan Am's downfall can be argued over and over again, but I think there were three major causes: first, worldwide competition and virtually no domestic support system; second, a wasteful and high-handed management; and third, and sadly, international terrorism.

It was said that Pan Am "cannot go under," like the *Titanic*. It was too big and too well established. It was to remain the "financially troubled Pan Am" for many, many years. Still, you worried about whether you were going to have a job the next day. And yet even in the end, after Delta Air Lines had bought the European routes, we believed that Pan Am would continue flying to South America and Central America as a smaller carrier. It was to be called Pan Am II. Delta also believed it would work, and there may have been or could have been a "feeding" to Delta's domestic system and a nice working partnership. In my own mind I had planned it that way and therefore decided to stay with Pan Am. Something in the back of my mind made me change course. I was interviewed by Delta and hired consequently and while in training in Atlanta got the shocking news. Only a month had gone by. Pan Am was no more, December 4, 1991. I could not believe it; none of us could believe it. What happened to the South American routes, what about Pan Am II, and what about the employees? The employees who had elected to stay with Pan Am. It was highly unfair. They were never warned. Contrary to high-level management, who got away with golden parachutes or fat bonuses or million-dollar salaries, the rank and file were on the street.

Somebody had decided to shut Pan Am down—for whatever reason. There was no money, it was said. It had been wasted or embezzled. Delta could not help Pan Am anymore. A billion-dollar lawsuit was to follow against Delta lasting a few years, spurred by the Pan Am creditors and others, who wanted their money. They claimed that Delta had been instrumental in causing the demise of Pan Am. Justice prevailed. Delta won the lawsuit by proving the contrary. I believe that Pan Am would be flying today if somebody had not decided to shut it down so hastily but instead had taken the time to work with the Delta management and create a South American and North American feeder route system. It is possible, of course, that everybody acted in good faith, or thought they did. However, I still don't think they tried hard enough. If you had asked the now suddenly jobless thousands if they would try hard enough, the outcome certainly would have been different. Why did Pan Am have to fold?

If you go back in history, it was, foremost, the competition that was encroaching upon Pan Am's enviable route system, as Pan Am, strangely complacent, in its arrogance did not pay heed. We flew around the world and in and out of remote areas like Pago Pago in the Pacific or Baghdad in Iraq or Nairobi in Kenya, never mind these routes were not profitable. Who cared about "other" airlines? We were not in it for the profit motive; we were the premier U.S. flag carrier and terribly proud of it. We were living off our legend. We were serving our Sevruga caviar and setting out the starched white linens and china in first class along with pale orchids on every tabletop. We set the standards, and we were haughty. Who cared about competition? What a mundane word!

But the decline had started. Flying was no longer a privileged domain. Along with the 747 came everybody. Along with deregulation came cheaper fares and cheaper airlines, who started to fly on "our" routes. How dared they! "They" certainly did not know how to do a first-class service with flair, let alone with sterling silver and folded linen napkins shaped like flowers!

Pan Am failed to adapt to a changing flying world. It was not only the low-fare carriers or even the other American airlines that threatened Pan Am. It was formidable competition from international British Airways, Singapore Airlines, and Lufthansa. Those airlines were more innovative than Pan Am and much more aggressive in the marketplace. Pan Am was very complacent indeed. But in a way, that's what was so charming about flying for Pan Am. For many years we just flew and flew and carried on "business as usual" and liked it. Everyone was roaring around us, but we just went our merry way, doing what we had always done—shopping in Rome, dinner in Frankfurt, massage in Tokyo, swimming in the ocean by the beach in Monrovia—and working understaffed on the airplane but still delivering a reasonably good service.

The American carriers that started to compete with us internationally had gigantic domestic route systems.

Pan Am had virtually none of that. We had coast-to-coast flights and little else. With no feeder system, we could not compete effectively.

So Pan Am acquired National Air Lines in the early eighties. It was at first a disaster. The intermingling of the work force and routes and schedules and managements was disorganized and unplanned. There was friction for years between employees and too much money wasted, which Pan Am could not afford. The decline went further. That buyout of National was probably a mistake, simply because it cost too much with too little compensation.

Which brings us to the Pan Am management, historically high-handed and arrogant—and wasteful. This, I believe, was the second reason for Pan Am's downfall.

According to a *Condé Nast Traveler* report in July 1991, by author Peter Wilkinson "Brigadier General William Seawell came in with a brisk, imperial manner. . . . Formal and difficult to approach. . . . Seawell flew first-class and loathed having to speak directly to a flight attendant. His wife Judith became meddlesome and oversaw the design of a new flight attendant uniform. He was the 'General,' one employee remembered, and 'she was the Generaless.' "

When Seawell was CEO in the midseventies, at first business improved for a little while. He laid off employees and adjusted routes. He evaded bankruptcy, but there was still no long-term strategy. Pan Am costs were way too high, overburdened by the cost of the 747s and unable and unwilling to adapt to a changing marketplace. Management always seemed to make excuses: fuel prices were too high (so they were for all the airlines), labour costs were too high, the employees were the problem, which often was a familiar refrain (we had given concessions year after year after year), and there was, finally, no domestic feeder route system.

So Seawell then made the one decision that injured Pan Am more than any other. He bought National Airlines for $432 million. This created incredible labour problems, disruptions in flight schedules, etc. I remember the airline was suddenly divided into blue and orange lines, and there was much animosity. According to the above article, "What possessed the General? Perhaps it was pathological Pan Am egotism. Seawell had been among the first to bid for National. When the two other airlines made offers, he became like a covetous art lover at Christie's. He could not stop bidding. The $432 million Pan Am paid was twice National's book value—overpriced under any circumstances, outrageous in light of deregulation."

Pan Am paid dearly for its mistake. It was slowly being dismembered. In 1981 Seawell sold the Pan Am Building on Park Avenue for $400 million and the Inter-Continental Hotels for $500 million. But we still did not have any cash!

Then came Acker. C. Edward Acker had owned Air Florida, was a savvy businessman who could borrow money easily, and viewed the airline business as a chess game (like others at the time, e.g., Lorenzo of Eastern Air Lines and Icahn of TWA): "He was always wheeling and dealing."

At first we were "Acker Backers." He was "down-to-earth," supposedly, and when he entered the offices of Pan Am would ask, "Who's in charge here?" There were few followers in Pan Am, mostly leader types, and everybody "did their own thing"!

Acker managed to change things around somewhat, cut costs by replacing some planes with more fuel-efficient airbuses, plane interiors were redesigned, menus were changed—but somehow we still were not saving any money. It was like one step forward and two steps backward. Acker ordered sheepskin seats for first-class seats, but what was the point of doing that when the rest of the airplane had leaky galleys and toilets and soiled carpeting, inoperative audio systems, broken latches everywhere, malfunctioning seat backs and tabletops, and other faulty maintenance items all over those planes that were written up in the logbooks over and over again, flight after flight, and never corrected properly? Also, there was the aforementioned costly netting for the overhead bins which was never completed. Soon enough, even the sheepskins in first class started to look worn and dirty.

At JFK, Pan Am was being overcharged for everything. I remember story after story about Pan Am being billed for catering items that were never brought on board and how the bills were falsified, the allegedly Mob-controlled trucking industry charging Pan Am three times more than other airlines. As I mentioned earlier, it would cost fifteen dollars for an extra lemon! Why? Because there was poor overseeing or leadership or supervision. People were on the take all over the system. The stealing on the ground at JFK was rampant; the liquor provisions would be cleaned out after the arrival of a flight. There were jokes about Jamaica Bay being filled with miniature bottles. There were stories about kickbacks and payoffs for favors and people being "upgraded" to first class for a fee under the table. There were infamous tales about pursers on board the airplane, who would collect the empty economy miniature bottles, fill them up again with first-class liquor from large bottles, and resell them again in economy for quite a profit at three dollars a bottle. The cabin headsets were also never accounted for.

Then Acker sold the Pacific routes to United Air Lines

in 1985 for (only) $750 million. We were just out of cash and needed the money to survive. Many people thought that that was a death knell to Pan Am. However, I remember how close we were to bankruptcy. I sort of believe that this move enabled Pan Am to survive a little longer. I don't think Pan Am could have survived in the long run flying the Pacific anyway. Although these were profitable routes, Pan Am management was still too wasteful. Now, what happened to the $750 million? Again, it was spent without paying off the debts and, more important, Pan Am's underfunded pension obligations, waived by the IRS! Acker bought the Pan Am shuttle with some of the money, but as a former executive said, "We could have used the money to make the airline better, to emphasize the rest of Pan Am."

Employee morale had hit bottom by now. Not only had management wasted money and made many wrong decisions through the years, but they had had the nerve to wring concessions out of the employees year after year, no small amounts either—we are talking about up to 25 percent pay cuts and frozen pensions (by Acker in 1984) without *ever* giving up one single penny of their own million-dollar salaries and parachutes, which were increased by themselves year after year!

Acker's lifestyle came under attack, and Pan Am board members always flew free in first class and collected huge salaries for doing absolutely nothing to help the airline.

According to an article in *Business Week* of March 1985 (reprinted by permission):

A recent study by Lazard Freres & Co. shows that Pan Am is likely to run out of cash by mid-1986, unless costs are cut drastically. Have we a classic case of Pan Am management cutting off their noses to spite their faces? Workers on the other hand view it as we see it, that they are being made scapegoats for management's failures, a cynical plan to blame labour. . . . Pan Am had blundered away $50 million last year because management needlessly placed a deadline on the frequent traveler program, the result being that in peak season full-paying passengers could not book seats. . . . If managerial incompetence is the underlying issue, managerial arrogance brought matters to a head. Last summer, Acker unilaterally froze worker pension plans in seeming violation of existing contracts. Why is Pan Am out of step? Lazard suggests its problems reflect its history, in which management downplayed the profit motive in favor of emphasizing its role as the premier U.S. flag carrier.

If management waste and arrogance had always been an underlying negative syndrome at Pan Am—and it was amazing how long we lasted in spite of that—another much more dire and tragic problem had started to beset the prime U.S. flag carrier all over the world. I think international terrorism finally did us in.

Pan American with its prominent American features and that beautiful blue ball on its airplanes, flying all over the world, Africa, the Middle East, the Far East, Europe, and South and Central America, was a target for terrorists that started a long time ago. Pan American World Airways *WAS* the United States of America—most certainly in the eyes of potential terrorists, young anti-American students all over the world. Pan Am also represented power, wealth, and American glamour and, loosely, the Establishment, which a lot of disturbed antisocial individuals enjoyed attacking verbally. I remember as far back as 1966, when I lived in Teheran for six months before being hired by Pan Am, how some of the young Iranians I was meeting at parties, and so forth, were sneering at anything American and so blatantly criticized the whole Western world. It had been the same when I had been in Paris a year earlier. It was always the Algerians or other students of Arabian origin who would never stop talking about all the ills of Western society and the United States in particular. I think they were part of the background for international terrorism that started to threaten the airline industry a little later in the early seventies. The attacks on Pan Am in the ensuing years were many.

People have already forgotten a lot of what happened to Pan Am during the seventies and the eighties. As they say, the public has a short memory. Long before the Lockerbie tragedy that ultimately broke Pan Am for good, there was the terrorist attack on the ground in Karachi, where many Indian and Pakistani passengers died. There was the Rome attack on the open runway, a grenade fired into the first-class section. There was a terrible incident after take-off in San Francisco, where a Japanese boy was severely injured by an explosive device under his seat.

There were bomb threats all the time. The only other airline that suffered almost as many attacks was TWA, another high-profile international American airline.

Several times out of JFK, I remember, we had to interrupt boarding passengers because of bomb threats, most of them hoaxes. All the different security measures we lived by were emphasized all the time and changed accordingly through the years.

We were instructed from time to time to keep a very low profile when in uniform walking through the airline terminals all over the world and in hotel lobbies, even to the point of not staying together but walking separately and even covering up the uniform with a civilian coat.

The crew buses that picked us up at the airport

frequently took different routing to avoid possible terrorists attacks. And that was no joke. In Teheran at one time just before the taking of the American hostages there, when the crew bus was just about to leave the crew hotel with the crew on board, a crowd of Iranians attacked it and started to shake it back and forth, shouting anti-American slogans at the crew. After that, there were to be no signs of the Pan Am logo on crew buses.

On the airplane for a while it was our job to check the seats and overhead bins and the toilets and the galleys for suspicious articles, just like the security personnel are doing today professionally. We resented having to lift the seat cushions and find something there. There would have been no protection. And that was at a time when there was a tremendous amount of terrorist activity although mainly hijackings.

We were always on the lookout for suspicious behaviour by passengers. We would report anything unusual to the captain or the station manager at whatever station we were flying out of, usually during the boarding process. Now and then passengers were offloaded with more or less turmoil by security personnel. However, there was much less security at that time, and it was less strict. It took far too many tragedies for the different governments and the FAA and the airlines to wake up and do something serious about it. Also, the bags in the cargo compartment were never scanned properly. Only sometimes, when a passenger was missing at boarding time, the flight could be delayed for a few hours, because his belly-loaded suitcase had to be searched—but not always. The flight would often leave anyway. Security was spotty and so lax that I, for one, felt that it was like Russian roulette. During the worst years you breathed a sigh of relief after every flight lucky to be alive. Even the pilots said that. "It's a dangerous job, but someone has to do it," I remember one saying. "If it wasn't an engine fire on one of the 747s or a bomb threat upon boarding or some other happening . . . A lot of HD!" we used to say. High Drama.

Yes, security was a great concern to those of us who took notice. The security personnel were called Alert, introduced by management at very low cost. They were poorly trained—only a few days—and supposedly paid minimum wage! These people were responsible for your life! "What a joke," we used to say. The scanners would spend far too long watching the screens, and the others would stand around chatting with each other, barely motioning you through indifferently.

Just like the death of President Kennedy, we all remember where we were and what we were doing. *On December 21, 1988, Pan Am flight 103 crashed in Lockerbie, Scotland in the early evening.* I was just about to pick up a new uniform at the Pan Am grooming center at JFK Airport. My friend was downstairs waiting in the car. I said I would only be a minute. When I walked into the uniform place, I could not understand why the lady at the desk there looked at me so gravely. "Don't you know," she said, "the 103 has crashed . . . just after taking off from London?"

"Where? How? Why?" I gasped. First I felt anger, because I honestly believed it had to be another engine failure.

"It was a London crew," she continued. "They don't know what happened. . . . "

I picked up my uniform items silently and then walked out of there, tears streaming down my face. I never thought about a bomb at that time. It had to be one of those damn engines. Who were the crew members? Did I know any of them? I cried in the car. My friend was silent and sympathetic and sort of world-wise, which was his trade-mark. The crew was my family, they were Pan Am, it was a personal, absolutely devastating loss. I soon found out who they were. I had flown with two of them, and I knew the captain. The faces on their pictures published later looked all so familiar. It could have happened to any one of us in Pan Am, but they were the unlucky ones.

The Lockerbie tragedy was to be the worst terrorist incident in U.S. aviation history, and those responsible still have not been brought to justice.

Pan Am never recovered. Twenty-five percent of the bookings fell.

People would say, "I'll fly any airline but Pan Am. . . . "

Now every time I see that picture of the broken blue-and-white cockpit sideways in the Scottish field with the lettering, the name of that airplane, *Maid of the Seas,* I hold back the tears.

20

1991 and Still Loving That Blue Ball

"PAN AM CONTINUES—1991," I have written next to the latest samples of in-flight snapshots in my picture album, although "under Chapter 11?!" The pictures show interiors of the cockpit and the cabin with passengers in the blue seats, smiling crew members sitting and standing and a closeup of the first-class credenza table with the white folded linen napkin in a stemmed glass and two gleaming coffeepots and sugarbowl and creamer all in silver.

We still had style, first-class style, and the food was the best and the freshest in the sky.

We were still very much family, maybe more than we had ever been. Also, during the last years from the end of the eighties there was less animosity towards management and a much calmer environment in Pan Am. This was due in part to our new chairman, Tom Plaskett, and along with him there appeared briefly a glimmer of hope of restoring Pan Am to its former glory. Well, some of us were dreaming. Plaskett promised another "new era" at Pan Am: "Our future can be every bit as bright as those days when the Pan Am name was legendary."

However, Pan Am's London routes were suddenly sold to United Air Lines, again one more jewel gone. All of the Pan Am employees, the flight attendants, at that station had to go to United, and they were in for some battle. They were placed at the bottom of the seniority list at United and at half their former pay. After the struggles and givebacks with Pan Am, that was a punch in the stomach. (Later, however, they regained most of their seniority and pay and are now doing fine.)

After the Lockerbie incident, Plaskett tried to change course and tried very hard to avoid leading Pan Am into extinction. He made a daring move, and if that move had succeeded, we would surely be flying today. It was very clever. He pursued Northwest Air Lines in 1989 with a $3.5 billion bid, backed by a syndicate of banks. The two airlines together would have become the biggest airline in the USA, and Pan Am would have regained the Pacific market. He almost made it. I remember that he flew all the way to Tokyo and stayed awake for a few days and nights talking to Northwest. But it failed and cost Pan Am $28 million.

We liked Plaskett. He was mild-mannered and approachable and came around to talk to us in the crew lounges and answer questions. Acker we had watched on the video screen talking in a monotone drawl, and Seawell we never ever saw a glimpse of, except in first class. Brian Moreau, our formidable union leader at the time, said that the employee morale was then "as good as it ever has been" and "it's the camaraderie you see when you're in the last lifeboat and you're bailing."

We were down to our last $30 million and in Chapter 11.

As before, just to raise cash and stay alive Pan Am had to sell something more. It became the valuable internal German division, the IGS, that was sold to Lufthansa for only $150 million—far less than the asking price. And the London routes had been sold to United for $290 million. We had been in Germany since World War II and in Britain for fifty-two years.

We were still losing $2 million a day. The 747s were in terrible shape across the Atlantic and were now being replaced by the new fuel-efficient European airbuses.

Pan Am needed a partner, a merger. The World's Most Experienced Airline's route system was unequaled and attractive and worth a lot! The significant year of 1991 had arrived with trepidation. Pan Am was bankrupt. The Gulf War had now broken out, and we were volunteering to fly the troops to and from Saudi Arabia. I had had many civilian flights before to Dhahran. While on layovers there we were required to cover up our bodies from top to toe in loosely fitting garments, even covering the arms and necks. At the hotel pool, no bikinis had been allowed, so we put on our one-piece bathing suits dutifully and mixed only with other women and children. Men had different hours reserved at the pool. We also ate our meals in special areas, and absolutely no alcohol was ever permitted anywhere in Saudi Arabia, although it was rumoured that wine was being home-made and whiskey was served at the U.S. embassy and other places. The Arabic women on the way to New York would board in their *chador* and halfway through the flight the veils would come off and they would also be seen drinking. On the way back to Dhahran the exact opposite took place.

This time I did not have such a great desire to go there again with Scud missiles all around. I left that to the more adventuresome and younger crew members. After all, I had had my share in Vietnam twenty years earlier. However, I volunteered to take an incoming flight from Rome through New York and on to North Carolina. It was the Eighty-second Airborne Division of paratroopers I had the honor of accompanying back to their base. It was the fifteenth of March, towards the end of Desert Storm. I never saw so many guns and battle gear and paraphernalia in the cabin. This was a 747, and the overhead bins and under seats were stuffed with all this. Most of these young guys were cheerful, happy to be home soon, and they did not mind relating their experiences and voicing opinions about the war. There was also a lot of sand all over! Desert sand. One of them held up *Time* magazine, and sure enough, there was his picture—on the cover!

A few years later I received in the mail, to my great surprise, an envelope from the air force. Inside was a great big navy blue certificate, stating that I had been awarded the civilian Desert Shield and Desert Storm medal for "outstanding achievement" and along with that a real medal with a ribbon. We had been part of "The CRAF personnel—flight crews and ground personnel—who entered the theater at least once between August 2, 1990, and April 11, 1991, eligible to receive the medal."

After the Gulf War ended, fuel prices dropped and people began flying again, but Pan Am still could not attract enough travellers to make money, not even during the upcoming summer. The Pan Am name was too closely associated with terrorism. Desert Storm had not helped. Every day was iffy; did we have a job? Would we get a partner? Who? As flight attendants, we did not want United, because our former colleagues had lost so much seniority with them (later adjusted). American or Delta Air Lines looked better. However, American had a union, so they would probably place us at the bottom also, if we were ever hired. Would the important routes be sold with or without the employees? Would we be totally dismantled? Chopped up in pieces and be awarded to different airlines? As the summer approached, it looked like United would become the new megacarrier, swallowing us minus our glorious history. But instead a bidding war erupted among United, Delta, American, and even TWA.

Delta emerged the big winner, from an opening bid of $260 million to $310 million and finally $416 million, too little for some and a little too much for others. I think Delta was favoured, because they cleverly gave $80 million to keep Pan Am operating, showed willingness to help the remaining Pan Am, as well as promised to hire many of the employees. The remaining Pan Am would be called Pan Am II and fly only to South America and Central America, based in Miami, sort of Pan Am's origin area. This happened in August 1991. Delta began immediately to operate the former Pan Am shuttle at La Guardia Airport's Marine Air Terminal in September.

I was hired by Delta and signed with them September 20 after being interviewed the twenty-ninth of August as well as language-tested in three languages and medically cleared. Of course it was a great relief, especially since I had almost decided to remain with Pan Am and suddenly had changed my mind.

Delta had wanted Pan Am's European routes (and the East Coast shuttle) and along with that our multilingual flight attendants, never mind we were on average quite a bit more senior than the average Delta flight attendant. They had also started to hire from the top on down, which, I have to admit, showed a certain respect for age! We were experienced, that's for sure!

November 1 was D day, I called it. Over to Delta, and a new world. While I was in training in Atlanta, the news came as a thunderbolt. We simply could not believe it! Pan Am was no more! December 4, 1991, the grand tradition was over. The Pan Am style of flying we would never see again.

On September 16 the *Wall Street Journal* carried an

article on its front page titled "Lost Horizons: A Grand Tradition Can Make a Fall That Much Harder. For Pan Am Employees, Fate of Airline They Loved Brings Stress and Depression" (reprinted from *The Wall Street Journal*, September 16, 1991).

The article starts out like this:

Pan American World Airways was once considered the queen of aviation, and its employees were among the industry's elite. At what other carrier could a flight crew have lunch in Pago Pago on Monday, breakfast in Los Angeles on Tuesday and then spend two days shopping in London before jetting off to Frankfurt on Friday? What other airline would reserve a swank little hotel in Monrovia, on the West Coast of Africa, just for its jumbo-jet crews? In the 1970's the allure of a job with Pan Am was so great that the carrier could choose its flight attendants from among thousands of applicants. Those lucky enough to sign on became ambassadors to the world. "No other job on the planet would allow us to duplicate our life style," says Brian Moreau, president of Pan Am's Independent Union of Flight Attendants. "That created a lot of loyalty." But today Pan Am is a shadow of its former self—a victim of management mistakes, a turbulent world economy and U.S. airline deregulation favoring carriers with strong domestic route systems.

It then continues:

Pan Am's glamour didn't count for much. In Chapter 11 proceedings since January, the company recently agreed to sell most of its assets to Delta Air Lines. . . . still hopes to operate the airline as a scaled-down carrier, the chances are remote that Pan Am will ever regain even a glint of its former glory. Such upheaval would be painful for employees at any company. But for Pan Am people, the experience has been especially traumatic, because the carrier fell from such heights. . . . Many workers report that they began to suffer severe emotional distress. . . . Personal problems have increased . . . pilots, among others, say they have had trouble concentrating on their work. . . . Stress-related safety concerns, . . . flight crews internalize stress . . . but it's there.

"These people are experiencing extremely deep grief," according to a doctoral candidate in counseling at Cornell University. "Many," she says, "have constant headaches, insomnia and digestive problems, that may reflect depression."

According to the article there had even been some suicides and heart attacks.

"Our blood runs blue," was one company slogan. There was such love for the airline. In April 1975, just days before North Vietnamese troops seized Saigon, a group of Pan Am pilots and flight attendants volunteered to fly into the city and rescue 363 of the airline's employees and family members.

The article ends by quoting a former Pan Am pilot who says, in spite of his accumulated medical problems due to the demise of Pan Am: "It's been a great life and career with Pan Am." Or to quote another: "The days when working for Pan Am was one of the best goddamn jobs in the world."

My very last flight with Pan Am was #23 to San Francisco and then back again to New York on #22 on October 27, 1991. The circle had closed. San Francisco was where it all started. That's where I flew my first flight in 1966, to Tokyo, all ten hours, working the back galley of the 707, all smeared with gravy over my smock and nervous of making mistakes, surviving and conquering my airsickness!

Now, in 1991, I was in charge as first-class purser on the airbus, still loving that blue ball. The crew was wonderful, sweet old friends of mine. There was Rita, excellent in the cabin and very meticulous, always folding those darn linen napkins and insisting upon properly laid "serviettes." "Amy," she said to me, "it has to be *neat!*" With us was Barbara, who worked the galley, while she was singing parts from musicals. She really was a singer, singing in professional groups. On the way back from San Francisco, during the dishing up of individual breakfast items on the first-class plates, she would sing in a clear pearly voice, "We say 'tomatoes,' you say 'tomatoes,' we say 'potatoes . . . '" Those first-class plates looked yummy! I will never forget it. I was laughing so hard in the galley and smiling from ear to ear when walking out in the cabin with my silver coffeepot.

That layover in San Francisco was memories all over again. I had only recently been flying back there on the coast-to-coast flights, which I had started to like in order to get away from the European jet lag. I had always had time-change problems with Europe, which had not been the case with going the other way. Tokyo had always been easier for me, as well as the Pacific flying.

We had almost two days in San Francisco, and how we used that time! Shopping in Chinatown, where I acquired one whole six-foot floor screen with wildflowers on it in green and black and pink, a very beautiful lacquer vase, several other little Chinese ornaments, carefully selected with Rita along to select and spend endless time discussing the qualities of these, or lack thereof. It really was exquisite fun to shop with Rita. Every little detail was very important. Then there were visits to Union Square, more shopping at the exclusive department stores, rides on the old cable cars, although much more crowded than they used to be and more expensive! We HAD to go to Japantown and have sushi and sake, and so we did. It was great fun, just like the good old days.

Afterword

I have a tape. It's a tape about the Pan Am story, titled *Death of an American Dream*. It was made after Pan Am's fall. It is quite good and well made. Some of the opinions demonstrated there I agree with and some I don't quite. Pan Am was not just a job, it was a state of mind, and like the song:

Pan Am has a place of its own
You call it the World; we call it Home

Capt. Mark Pyle flew the last Pan Am flight into Miami's International Airport on December 4, 1991, and in the air was asked to do a "low pass" onto the runway, this after being informed of the devastating news. A low pass was at 100 feet and at 180 knots, and after briefing passengers, they landed on runway 12 with the fire trucks all around and the water cannons spraying the 727 airplane from the sides in cascades. He said at that point it was difficult to get to the gate, every eye tearful. On the tape he is interviewed, and this is what he says:

> She was like an elegant, majestic lady, who, in the years of her glory, was very beautiful ... and then towards the end of her existence, when she wasn't so beautiful any more, she was put up to auction, like a slave ... and she was stripped of her clothing ... one garment at a time, the Pacific, the Pan Am building, the IGS, etc. until she stood

153

there naked . . . before they could sell the final piece, she simply died of shame . . . an elegant lady now of history . . . what a grand lady she was in her time!